HARD RIDE TO LARGO

When Jack Danner arrived in Haley Ridge he spent the night in jail. But then financier Spencer Bonnington offers him fifteen hundred dollars to escort Sarah, his niece, to her father's ranch in Largo. However, their journey is fraught with danger, especially when Bob Rand and his partners see Sarah as a prize and a means of ransom from the Bonningtons. Danner is being watched, but by whom? An easy fifteen hundred becomes the hardest money he's ever earned.

Books by Jack Holt
in the Linford Western Library:

GUNHAWK'S REVENGE
PETTICOAT MARSHAL
HOT LEAD RANGE

JACK HOLT

HARD RIDE TO LARGO

Complete and Unabridged

LINFORD
Leicester

First published in Great Britain in 2006 by
Robert Hale Limited
London

First Linford Edition
published 2008
by arrangement with
Robert Hale Limited
London

British Library CIP Data

Holt, Jack
    Hard ride to Largo.—Large print ed.—
Linford western library
    1. Western stories
    2. Large type books
    I. Title
    823.9'2 [F]

    ISBN 978-1-84782-051-8

Published by
F. A. Thorpe (Publishing)
Anstey, Leicestershire

Set by Words & Graphics Ltd.
Anstey, Leicestershire
Printed and bound in Great Britain by
T. J. International Ltd., Padstow, Cornwall

This book is printed on acid-free paper

1

'Your luck just ain't in, mister,' the man seated across the table from Jack Danner chuckled, his soft, well-manicured hands reaching for the blackjack pot. 'Sometimes it just goes like that.'

'Well, now,' Danner drawled lazily, 'I guess it always goes like that when you're dealing, friend.'

There was instant tension round the table. The gambler feigned innocence. 'I'm not sure what you're implying, sir,' he said, his tone edgy.

'Then I'll make myself perfectly clear,' Jack Danner said, still in a lazy drawl. 'You're cheating.'

Chairs scraped on the saloon floor as the other men at the table slid away, leaving clear space between the gambler and Danner.

'That's a mighty charge to level,' the gambler said, his hands drifting away from drawing in the pot to the edge of the table. 'You're just a lousy card-player, mister.'

'Ain't much skill to blackjack,' Danner observed. 'You get the cards or you don't. And sometimes the cards which are your due, kind of end up where they darn well should not be.' Danner's unflinching grey eyes locked with the gambler's. 'Like that ace that was about to join my king, before you put it with your queen.'

'You're a bad loser,' the gambler ranted.

'You've got hands faster than a rattler's spit,' Danner said. 'Now I suggest that you return to me and these other fine gents, every cent you robbed from us. And then make tracks as fast as your nag will take you.'

By now the entire saloon crowd were waiting for the inevitable gunplay, most relishing the break in the nightly routine in a saloon that seldom saw action, in a town that suited the saloon.

'I won the money fairly,' the gambler protested.

'No, you didn't,' Danner countered.

The gambler's right hand dropped below the table. Danner upended the table forcefully, sending the gambler tumbling backwards off his chair. As swift as a mountain cat pouncing on a meal, the rangy Danner was round the upturned table and had the gambler by the shirt. He hauled him to his feet and hit him hard. The gambler shot across the saloon scattering its patrons every which way and crashed against the far wall. Before he could regain his wits, Jack Danner was on him again and landed a second jaw-buster. The gambler spun out of control and reeled about the saloon. Willing hands shoved him back into the arena which had formed in the middle of the floor, and straight into a third pile-driver from Danner. The gambler crashed heavily against the bar, and when Danner followed to wade in again, the gambler held his hands up and cowered like a whipped puppy.

'I'll give everyone their money back,' he whined.

'You're getting off lightly. Most towns would hang you,' Danner reminded the gambler. He turned to his fellow card players. 'Say what you lost.'

The other men gladly reeled off their losses, most adding a couple of dollars.

'You're still owing,' he told the gambler, when the pot had been divided.

The gambler gladly handed over the roll of dollars in his coat pocket. Refunds made good, Jack Danner stalked out of the saloon.

'Look out!' came the cry from behind him.

Danner swung round and threw himself aside as a stiletto whizzed past to imbed itself in the batwings just behind him. His sixgun flashed from leather. The gambler was caught cold. Danner teased the Colt's trigger, his anger white hot. He had given the gambler every chance, and in return the bastard had tried to kill him.

4

The crowd drifted to the four corners of the saloon, leaving the gambler alone, the sole occupant of the centre of the saloon, awaiting certain death.

'Please, mister,' the gambler pleaded. 'For God's sake don't kill me.'

Sweat as thick as treacle covered the gambler's face, and the most awful shakes took hold of him. Jack Danner's reason kicked in to assuage his anger. Justified as he would be in taking his revenge by the code of the West, killing the gambler would in essence be murder. Surprise was the order of the day when Jack Danner holstered his sixgun.

'Just clear out!' he growled.

'Sure, mister,' the gambler croaked. 'Thanks, mister.'

He went past Danner in a stumbling run on legs that were like jelly, out of the saloon. Seconds later a fast horse thundered out of town.

'Should've killed him!' a man bellied up to the bar growled.

'Why?' Jack Danner questioned the

man. 'Everyone got what was their due.' Danner looked at the grim faces around the saloon, and saw that the man who had spoken his thoughts was voicing what most of the others had wanted.

'He'll only repeat his cheatin' in another town down the line,' the man at the bar said.

'Then let someone in that town kill him,' Danner responded, stony-faced. He turned to leave the saloon. 'My business with that gent and this town is over. Got a hotel?' he enquired of the barkeep.

'Of sorts,' was the 'keeper's grumpy reply.

'If the bugs are smaller than a cat, it'll do,' Danner said, and continued his stride to the batwings.

'Coward!'

Jack Danner paused mid-stride, his back going rigid on hearing the slur. He turned slowly to face the youngster who had stepped clear of the crowd which was hurriedly dividing either side of him, opening up a space in the middle of the bar, the lad the new occupant of what had been the gambler's stand. Likewise, patrons behind and to either side of Danner edged away.

'Yella coward!'

'You tell him, Danny,' a voice called out from the crowd. 'You tell him good.'

The youngster called Danny was flushed with too much liquor, giving him false bravado. Danner reckoned that he had been carried away on the wave of excitement generated by him taking the gambler to task, and then the mood of anti-climax when he had been satisfied with the gambler's apology and his willingness to refund what he had acquired by sleight-of-hand.

'Ain't you goin' to do somethin' 'bout me callin' you a damn coward, mister?' Danny challenged Jack Danner. He shifted his stance and his hand hovered over the spanking new .45 in an equally unblemished holster.

An expectant hush had fallen over the saloon as the seconds to what seemed an inevitable gunfight counted down.

'Push me and I'll kill you for sure, son,' Danner said quietly. 'I reckon that the gun on your hip is a new pin rig.'

'I'm fast,' Danny boasted. 'I got plenty of practice with my pa's gun.' His face tightened with anger. 'He was shot down in cold-blood by a no-good gambler, just like the one you let ride free as a bird just now. So you damn well draw, mister. Or I'll drop you right where you stand.'

'I can see that you're not going to listen to reason, boy.'

'I ain't no boy!' Danner's challenger roared. 'I'm eighteen years old, and man enough to kill you, you no-good saddle tramp.'

Danner eyed the man coldly. 'Maybe,' Danner said. 'But I doubt it.'

'I'm plenty fast. As you're 'bout to find out,' the youngster snarled.

'You tell him, Danny,' the same voice called out from the midst of the crowd.

Danner sighed. 'You call it.'

'I don't want or need no special favours,' Danny growled. 'I'm ready when you are.'

The saloon went completely still, no one even daring to draw breath. Eyes switched between Danner and his challenger, looking for the flicker of movement that would signal gunplay. Jack Danner waited, hoping to faze out the youngster by dragging out the wait. Hoping against hope that his young opponent would get sense from somewhere, while knowing from past experience that pride would probably overrule reason.

Tiring of the wait, the youngster shouted, 'Damn you!' and went for his gun.

His hand had not touched iron before he stood under threat of Jack Danner's sixgun, which had appeared in his hand as if by magic. The youngster paled, knowing that the stranger had every right now to kill him. He tensed, waiting for the bullet that would rip through him. His surprise was total when Danner again, as he had done with the gambler, showed mercy and reholstered his pistol.

'Ain't you goin' to kill me?' Danny asked, disbelievingly.

Danner shook his head. 'Learn from this,' Jack Danner told the youngster. 'Now go away and live a long and good life, son.' The young man ran from the saloon, shouting his thanks to Danner.

'What's wrong with this damn town,' he asked the saloon patrons, in disgust, 'that you'd goad a youngster in to throwing away his life?'

Jack Danner strode through the crowd to where the man was who had urged Danny on and brought his fist up from the floor into his gut. As he bent over, Danner brought his other fist up under the stirrer's chin and almost tore his head from his shoulders with the force of the blow. The man catapulted back into a corner of the saloon and slid down the wall to the floor. Danner settled an angry glare on the crowd, which melted away from him as he strode out of the saloon.

'The sooner I can shake the dust of this burg from my boots, the better I'll like it,' he said, turning, before crashing through the batwings into the night.

The hotel was at the far end of the main street; a street that was filled with shadows created by a fitful moon ducking between the rag ends of earlier storm clouds. Conscious of the ill-feeling that recent events had generated (he wasn't the most popular fellow in Haley Ridge right then), Jack Danner would have preferred a street lit by an uninterrupted moon, or alternatively a street without a hint of moonlight at all. With the former he could see every-thing, and with the latter pretty much nothing. But the stability of either condition would make any movement recognizable in good time. However, a street full of shifting shadows was a thoroughfare rife with danger, because any one of the shifting shadows could, in the blink of an eye, materialize into a man carrying a gun, or, more likely, a knife; knives were silent, and most often the choice of weapon for a man on a mission of stealth. Other than trouble emanating from the bad feeling his visit to the saloon had started, there was also the motive of robbery. Danner was aware of the sizeable poke in his pocket, his share of the gambler's ill-gotten gains. Haley Ridge was a town just about surviving. The shabbiness of the stores and dwellings was evidence of the town's hard times. Work would be as hard to find as water in the desert that encircled the town, encroaching more and more every day, reclaiming its own, as the citizens saw little point in trying to stave-off the desert's persistent march. In Jack Danner's opinion, it would not be long now before the sigh of Haley Ridge became a death-rattle. And right now, that meant that there were a lot of desperate men looking for another meal, or a stake to shake off the town's dust before they became part of that dust.

A lame horse had brought him to the town, and he was now regretting that he had not ridden out, on the new mare he had purchased from the livery. But the desert was long and arid and uninviting to a tired man. And it was late afternoon. So he had decided to stay the night. Now, looking along the deserted street — at least it looked deserted — Jack Danner hoped that his instincts would serve him well if the need arose. If they failed him, then he'd be staying in Haley Ridge for a whole lot longer than a night.

He began the long walk to the hotel, measuring his steps, pausing every now and then to listen and watch, and hugging the edge of the boardwalk as he passed any recessed doorways. He edged up to alleys and then, satisfied that there was no threat, he moved on quickly. A cat leapt from the overhang outside the general store and Danner's heart staggered.

'Should have slept under a table in the damn saloon,' he murmured.

He was almost to the hotel, which he reckoned would be the time of greatest danger. A bushwhacker would give himself all the time he could to watch the progress of his victim, and would figure that Danner's guard would drop more and more the nearer he got to the hotel. And in those last twenty yards or so, jittery, he would want to be rid of his anxiety and hurry along, less watchful.

'That was a load of old bullshit!' he said, turning in the door of the hotel, unthreatened. The dimly lit, shabby foyer, was about as welcoming as kissing a rattlesnake. The yellow parchment-faced clerk seemed to be as near to dying as did not matter. 'Got a room?'

The clerk looked at him tiredly. 'Got a whole building full of rooms, mister. Most empty.' The clerk turned the register towards him, creating a circle in the dust of the desk. 'Sign right here,' he instructed Danner.

Danner scrawled his name. The clerk turned the book back towards him, creating a circle within a circle in the dust.

'Mr Danner?' he checked, peering short-sightedly at the book.

'That's me,' Danner said.

The clerk reached behind him for a room key and placed it on the desk in front of Danner. Danner had a fleeting thought about why the clerk had chosen that key from an entire board of keys, but was too tired to ponder on the clerk's selection for longer than a second.

'How much is the room?' Danner asked, before he accepted the key.

'What're you offering?'

'What?'

'Business is kind of slow right now. It would normally be five dollars, but anything from two up will do.'

Danner placed two dollars on the desk. The clerk's bony hands grabbed it.

'Bath?' Danner enquired.

The clerk looked at him as if he had asked for his very soul to be surrendered.

'Breakfast?' Danner added, hopefully. The clerk positively shuddered.

'Sleep well and long, Mr Danner,' the clerk called after him as he went upstairs.

Jack Danner shook his head. He had seen many dead-end towns in his travels. But nothing as bereft of hope as Haley Ridge. He entered his room, still shaking his head, and felt a knife point at his throat. Now he knew why the clerk had selected the room key he had. There was nothing random about it. The knifeman had obviously arranged matters with the clerk before he had arrived. Clever.

'You bastard!' the gambler said. 'I'm going to slit your windpipe!'

2

Occasionally, in his thirty-six years, Jack Danner had had the odd regret, like now. And that regret was that he had shown the gambler mercy. If given the chance to redeem his error, he would not be of a mind to let the gambler off the hook again. Seeing that even the slightest movement would have the point of the blade piercing his throat, there was only one thing he could do, and even that would involve risk. He dropped his hand quickly, grabbed the gambler's testicles and squeezed with every ounce of strength that his cupped fist could muster. The gambler howled like a stricken animal — appropriate, Danner thought. Pressure at its full power, he twisted his wrist and the gambler's eyes almost popped clear out of his head. Danner shot his elbow back into the gambler's face and heard the satisfying snap of bone breaking as his nose was flattened to his face. A splinter of the shattered nose bone skewed off and buried itself in the gambler's right eye. Blood spurted instantly from the wounded eye. By now Danner was holding the man up. He turned, grabbed the pitiful looking gambler by the scruff of the neck, ran him across the room and threw him through the window. So forceful was Jack Danner's action, the gambler cleared the hotel porch overhang and crashed straight onto the street, his fall unbroken. He tried to get up, but his body collapsed in on itself, so many were his broken bones. He rolled over. Blood gushed from his gaping mouth. He whimpered and died. Quickly, Danner stepped through the window onto the roof of the overhang just as the desk clerk fled the scene of his treachery. Danner dropped down on him.

'Oh, sweet God, mister,' the clerk whined. 'He said he wanted to surprise you. I t-thought he was a f-f-friend, pulling a prank.'

'You lying toad!' Danner swore. 'I'm going to rip you apart bone by bone.'

'No you ain't.'

Danner turned on hearing the quiet voice, but though it was quiet, it held a note of steely resolve. He was looking into the barrels of a primed shotgun. While holding the cocked blaster on Danner with his right hand, the man used his left to flick open his waiscoat to reveal a star.

'Sheriff Jeb Scott,' he said. 'Just got back to town. Been hearing all about the goings on at the saloon.'

'Then you'll know that I've got right on my side, Sheriff,' Danner said. He pointed to the street. 'That passel of horseshit is the gambler who started all of this, and tried to end it just now by slitting my throat.'

'That's as maybe,' Scott said. 'But why're you figuring on killing Harry?'

' 'Cause the bastard set me up to have my throat slit.'

'It ain't true, Jeb,' the hotel clerk

pleaded. 'Like I told Mr Danner, I figured all the gambler wanted to do was surprise Mr Danner in a friendly but harmless way.'

'Then why were you lighting out like as if someone was holding a candle to your butt just now?' the sheriff barked.

'Because I knew that Mr Danner would think the wrong way, of course.'

Sheriff Jeb Scott sighed. 'If lying rotted a man's tongue, Harry Donovan, you'd be mute years ago.'

'Can I kill him now?' Jack Danner asked.

'Don't see why not,' Scott growled.

Harry Donovan's eyes held a wild fear.

'You just can't stand by and let Danner kill me, Jeb. What kind of a sheriff are ya?'

'Thanks, Sheriff Scott,' Danner said, and drew his gun. 'Shooting him will be quicker than breaking bones one by one.'

He cocked the pistol. Harry Donovan wobbled and passed out. He fell face down in his own urine. Jack Danner holstered his .45.

'He's all yours, Sheriff. Sure hope he's learned a lesson.'

'And where do you think you're going?' Jeb Scott asked, when Danner headed back inside the hotel.

'Bed.'

The shotgun came back up on Danner.

'You've killed a man.'

'Who tried to kill me first,' Danner said.

'Killing a man means lots of paperwork, and lots of questions. And you're going to jail until that paperwork is finished, and those questions have been asked and answered to my liking, Danner.'

Jack Danner let out a weary sigh.

'You know, Sheriff. I just wish I'd given this burg a wide berth.'

'Me, too,' Jeb Scott replied. He pointed the blaster. 'The jail is that way, so start walking, Mr Danner.'

'Ain't never been in jail before.'

'My sainted ma used to say that there's a first time for everything, Danner.'

Jack Danner began walking towards the jail. 'Bunks comfortable?'

'Lumpy as hell.'

'How about the coffee?'

'Tastes like mule's piss.'

'Do I get breakfast.'

'If you're quick enough to catch a passing fly.'

Jack Danner paused. 'You know, Sheriff, when you hand in that star, you might consider taking over running the hotel. With the kind of hospitable manner and experience you've got, it sure would be a natural move, I reckon.'

★ ★ ★

The night was long. The day ahead had all the makings of a bad one. That was until the excitement that hit town soon after sun-up.

3

'What in tarnation is it?' seemed to be the question on everyone's lips when the gold and silver stagecoach charged along the main street to draw rein in front of the hotel, its team of midnight black stallions straining at the leash.

'What're those ugly critters?' the awe-struck saloon swamper asked whoever might have the answer to his question. He pointed to the carved images on the four corners of the stagecoach roof.

'Gargoyles,' Alice Smithers, the schoolmarm, informed the swamper.

'What the heck are gar ... ? Gar — what did you say?'

'Goyles,' Miss Smithers said. 'Gargoyles.'

'Look like demons to me,' an old-timer sitting on the saloon porch observed. 'Sure wouldn't like to be bit on the ass by one. Sorry, ma'am,' he immediately apologized on seeing Alice Smithers' disapproving frown.

She's the spitting image of one of them gargoyles herself, the old-timer thought.

'Will you just look at that fancy inside, all plush red and gold uphol-stery,' the swamper said, when the driver opened the door of the stage and a young woman stepped out.

'Just like a darn palace on wheels, ain't it?' the old-timer said.

'And she looks like one of them princesses that are all the rage in Europe,' the swamper added.

The older man who accompanied her looked about him with a distinct scowl of distaste. 'Get back!' he ordered the crowd pressing round. He grabbed one man who came too close to the woman and shoved him aside. The man's boot caught on the edge of the boardwalk and he fell backwards. He sprang angrily to his feet, ready to challenge the expensively clad man.

A second man inside the stage, poked a pistol out of the window. A bullet nicked the toecap of the man's boot. He jumped back.

'He'll put the next bullet between your eyes,' said the man escorting the young woman.

'Put the gun away!' Sheriff Jeb Scott's order had the crack of a whip to it. 'Now, fella,' he told the man inside the stage, pointing the same shotgun at the stranger as he had at Jack Danner the night before.

The gunman took his instructions from the dudish man before responding to Scott's order.

'Sheriff . . . ?'

'Scott. Jeb Scott.'

The man proffered a hand to shake. 'Spencer Bonnington.' The Haley Ridge lawman ignored the proffered hand, and instead looked to the woman. 'May I introduce my niece Sarah, Sheriff?'

Jeb Scott touched his hat. 'Ma'am.'

The woman looked away, obviously not thinking that a small-town sheriff was of sufficient standing to be bothered with. She recoiled when the saloon swamper sniffed at her.

'Smells real purty,' he sniggered.

Spencer Bonnington slapped the swamper across the face.

'Get your filthy presence out of my sight!' he bellowed, his beefy face flushing with anger.

'Al didn't mean no harm, Bonnington,' the sheriff said in a no-nonsense tone. 'What did you expect, arriving in a small Western town in a rig like that? Not much happens round here. Most days just drift by, one into the next. Gets so that it's sometimes hard to know what day you're in, due to the fact that every day is the same.'

'Maybe I overreacted a touch,' Bonnington said.

'I'd say a whole pile,' Scott replied, stiffly.

Spencer Bonnington took a handful of silver dollars from his pocket and threw them to the swamper. 'I trust that that will compensate for my rash reaction.'

Al Brown's eyes popped on seeing the money.

'Buy your way out of most situations?' the sheriff enquired.

'It's been my experience that hurt and offence are readily assuaged by monetary compensation, Sheriff.'

'What lingo is he spoutin'?' the town blacksmith wondered, scratching his hairless head.

'From where do you hail, Bonnington?' Scott asked.

'Boston, now.'

'And before?'

'England, as a young man.'

'Explains the fancy lingo,' the blacksmith said.

'But I don't feel in anyway obliged to explain who I am, or the purpose of my visit, Sheriff,' Spencer Bonnington said haughtily.

'That a fact,' the Haley Ridge lawman drawled. 'Well, I guess it's about time we got some things straightend out, Bonnington. If I darn well ask, mister, you'd better darn well answer, and pronto. Understood?'

Bonnington's back went rigid.

'Understood?' Scott pressed, grim-faced.

'Perfectly, Sheriff. But I doubt if my friend the territorial governor would appreciate your attitude.'

'That a fact. Well, the next time you see the territorial governor, you tell him from me to go stick his head in a bucket!'

Spencer Bonnington bristled, but resisted the temptation to give the obvious spiky retort which had come to mind. Instead he said, 'My niece is rather tired.' He swept arrogantly past the sheriff and, under his hostile glare, the crowd parted.

'Thorny sorta fella,' the sheriff commented.

'You still got that feller Danner in the poky, Jeb?' a man enquired of the sheriff, when interest in Bonnington and his niece waned.

'I have, Ned.'

'A real tough *hombre*,' another man

said. 'The way he dealt with that gambler. Was right there in the saloon m'self. Seen ev'ry move.'

'You should have been at home with your wife, Eli,' Alice Smithers rebuked the man.

'Gotta be drunk 'fore I see her, or she scares the hell outa me, ma'am.'

The crowd broke into laughter.

'I declare Eli Grant, when God made you, he surely made his biggest mistake!'

As the schoolmarm flounced off, the laughter was even greater.

'Ya know,' Eli said, looking admiringly after the schoolteacher. 'Alice Smithers sure is one fine woman.'

Alice Smithers' step faltered slightly, and she pretended indifference to Eli Grant's remarks, but, as she went on, her shoulders were that bit straighter, and her head held that bit higher.

'Ya know, Eli,' Grant's sidekick said, 'maybe you should call round some night to the schoolmarm's door. I figure she's kinda stuck on you.'

'Darn it, Willie,' Eli exclaimed, 'I'm a married man.'

'Who never goes home sober,' Willie flung back.

'That don't mean that I can go callin' on other women, Willie. A man's got to have his standards, ya know.'

Willie was shaking his head. 'Wanna beer?'

Eli Grant licked dry lips. 'Can't say that I'd mind, Willie.'

'Well, come on then. At least when you're drunk, you don't talk as much horseshit as you do when you're sober.'

The crowd drifted away, and Sheriff Jeb Scott made his way back to the law office. On entering, Jack Danner hailed him.

'What was all the excitement about just now, Sheriff?'

'Some high-and-mighty honcho by the name of Spencer Bonnington rolled into town in a rig that would knock your eyes out. Caused a stir.'

'Spencer Bonnington?' Danner questioned.

'That's what I said,' the lawman confirmed. 'Know him?'

'Not personally. Only by reputation. Got more money than he could count in a month of Sundays. Big Boston financier is Spencer Bonnington.'

'How d'ya know all that, Danner?'

'Been to Boston. Worked for a spell as chucker-out at a swank watering-hole that served French food that you had to be able to read French to order. Spencer Bonnington used to often grub there. Folk treated him like God. And the big question that troubled everyone was, how the heck much Bonnington was worth.'

Jack Danner chuckled.

'Could buy this burg and the valley it sits in with the change in his pocket. Now, how about breakfast, Sheriff? I'm a tad hungry.'

'This ain't a damn hotel!' the sheriff groused.

'Neither is the hotel in this godfor-saken mistake of a town, a hotel. In fact, you should offer the jail as overnight accommodation to Bonnington before he gets his rich-as-Croesus ass eaten off by the bugs in the hotel. Upset, a critter like that could send a private army in here to burn the place to the ground.'

'I've heard enough about the high-and-mighty Spencer Bonnington,' the lawman growled. He grabbed the keys from a hook on the wall behind his desk and went and let Danner out of his cell. 'Go get your own damn breakfast!'

'You know, Sheriff, I might never come back to this town,' Danner said, strolling to the door.

'That's the best news I've heard in a long spell,' Scott said grumpily.

The morning was the kind that showed that God was in a good mood. The fresh breeze, a rare occurrence on the edge of desert country, got inside a man and revitalized him. It looked like the end of a long dry spell, if the storm clouds gathering on the burnished horizon kept coming their way. The fresher weather would not last for very long, but while it did men would become more affable and neighbourly and ready to see the other fella's point of view.

'Got an eaterie in this town?' Jack Danner asked a passer-by. The man pointed to a hash house further along the street on the opposite side. 'Obliged, sir.'

A little way on, the man turned and advised, 'Don't eat the eggs.'

'Why?'

The man held his stomach. 'Just don't, mister. I've been living in the privy since I did last week.'

'Probably just a bad batch.'

The man walked on, shaking his head and muttering. When Danner entered the Lazy Dog hash house, a tired and bored woman was saying, exasperatedly, to a man and a young woman, 'Of course you've got choice. You can have eggs, beans and bacon.'

'You've already said that,' the young woman said.

'No, I didn't,' said the woman,

presumably the proprietor and all-round dogsbody. 'I said that you could have eggs and beans. Never said nothin' 'bout bacon.'

'Eggs and bacon will do,' Spencer Bonnington barked. 'Never heard of a hotel that didn't serve breakfast.'

'Pull up a chair,' the woman told Danner. 'What'll it be?'

'What's good enough for Mr Bonnington is good enough for me, I guess,' Danner said.

The woman took a step back and let her eyes run over Danner's dusty and well-worn garb. 'Got the money to pay for it? I've already got more dish-washers than I need.'

'Why don't you join my niece and me for breakfast, sir,' Bonnington invited Danner.

'Really, Uncle Spencer!' his niece said, paling at the thought of having to share a table with the scruffily clad Jack Danner.

'It seems the gentleman and I have met before, Sarah my dear,' Bonnington said. 'Though where or how, I can't imagine.'

'I was a chucker-out at that fancy eating-house you used to go to in Boston,' Danner explained, pulling out a chair at the table. 'Do you still go there, Mr Bonnington?'

'Yes.' The financier patted his expanding belly. 'But not as often nowadays.'

'A chucker-out?' Sarah Bonnington said, seeking enlightenment from her uncle.

'A commissionaire, my dear,' he explained.

Sarah Bonnington's shock was complete, and her pallor deepened. She shifted her chair away from Jack Danner's, and her nostrils quivered.

'I guess I am a little on the ripe side,' Danner said, sniffing at himself.

'I fear, Uncle Spencer, that my appetite seems to have deserted me. I shall, with your permission, return to the hotel.' She stood up stiffly. 'Good day to you, sir.'

'You mustn't mind my niece, Mr —?'

'Danner. And I don't. Though I do think that a good spanking would do her a whole lot of good.'

'Yes. She has been rather spoiled, Mr Danner.'

'Kind of looks outa place, if you ask me.'

'The West is not to my niece's liking, Mr Danner.' Spencer Bonnington's lip curled sourly. 'Mine neither.'

'Which makes me kind of curious about why you're here?'

'My brother Nathaniel, Sarah's father, for some mysterious reason, ranches near Largo. Regrettably, mine is a mission of mercy, Mr Danner. You see, Nathaniel is dying. A tumour in his brain. Sarah is going to see him before he dies.

'Nathaniel lost his wife in childbirth, and he thought it best that Sarah should come and live with my wife and me in Boston. He wisely decided that this was too harsh a land for such a delicate flower to survive in. I agreed with him whole-heartedly. Mrs Bonnington and I have not been blessed with offspring. So it was indeed an arrangement that suited both sides. Sarah has only been back to see her father three times in all, the last visit was ten years ago when she was twelve years old.'

'That story tugs at the heartstrings, Mr Bonnington,' Danner said.

'Yes. It is rather a sad tale, isn't it?'

'She's lucky to have someone as caring as you,' Danner opined.

'That, sir, is very gracious of you to say so,' Bonnington said suavely.

Two plates of greasy food were plonked down on the table.

'Eat it while it's hot or it'll take a month to shift when it gets cold,' was the hash-house proprietor's cackling advice.

Spencer Bonnington looked at the excuse for food in horrified disgust.

'I have never seen such muck in all my life!' he bellowed.

'Still got to pay for it,' the proprietor said sternly.

Bonnington sprang out of his chair and threw the money on the table.

'Throw it to the dogs!' he barked,

and strode furiously out of the hash-house.

'Kinda picky, ain't he?' the proprietor said.

'Used to French food,' Danner said, transferring the contents of Bonnington's plate on to his.

'French food, huh!' the proprietor of the Lazy Dog hash-house snorted. 'And what's wrong with good old Western grub?'

'Not a thing, ma'am,' Jack Danner said, chewing on a strip of bacon, the grease from which ran down his chin, his tongue chasing it. His eyes rolled with pleasure. 'Not a darn thing.'

Jack Danner enjoyed his grease-laden meal, and was on his way out of town when his horse threw a shoe. The black-smith had gone on a bout of liquor-swilling, forcing Danner to remain another night in Haley Ridge — an occurrence which changed his plans.

4

Not relishing a stay in the hotel, Jack Danner struck a deal with the keeper to bunk down in the livery loft. The smell of hay and horse was not the most pleasing combination, but at least the bugs were not such blood-thirsty critters as they were at the hotel. As he settled down for the night, he wondered how a fat-wallet gent like Spencer Bonnington even considered staying in the excuse for a hotel. And the thought of his hoity-toity niece in bed with the voracious bugs, would make for pleasant dreams as he slipped into sleep, a sleep that was interrupted not long after it had begun by a loud rattling on the livery door.

'Jack Danner,' a man's gruff voice called out. 'You in there?'

'Cripes and holy shit!' the livery-keeper groaned. 'You didn't say your rowdy friends would be comin' by, Danner.'

The livery gates rattled again, fit to come crashing down so robust was the caller's attempt to gain entry.

'Danner!' the caller yelled.

'Answer the bastard,' the keeper shouted to the loft, 'before he brings the damn building down on us.'

'On my way,' Danner called back.

When he opened the livery gates, a man he recognized as the driver of Bonnington's stage growled, 'Mr Bonnington wants to see you.'

'That a fact,' Jack Danner responded spikily, not liking one little bit the driver's attitude.

'Right now!'

Danner's hackles were up. 'You go tell Bonnington that the morning will have to do, you hear?'

A Colt flashed in the driver's hand and prodded Danner's belly. 'Now, I said and now it's going to be, friend. Mr Bonnington is not a man who likes to be kept waiting.'

'Well, he's going to have to get used to it,' Danner said testily.

'If you don't walk right this second,' the driver threatened, 'I might just burn this hovel down.'

Up to that point, the livery-keeper had been approving of Jack Danner's independence, but with the livery at stake, he shifted sides quickly.

'Git!' he ordered Danner. 'You ain't welcome no more.'

'Looks like you're out on your ear, friend,' Bonnington's driver chuckled.

The livery-keeper shoved Danner out of the livery and quickly secured the gates.

'So why would Spencer Bonnington want to see me at' — he checked his pocket watch under the livery storm lantern — 'fifteen after midnight?'

'I guess he'll tell you that when you see him,' the driver stated.

A couple of minutes later, he did, but Bonnington first asked a question. 'You know this territory as far as the border, Danner?'

41

'Like my own backyard. If I had a backyard, that is.'

'I've got to return to Boston urgently,' he told Danner brusquely. 'Important business. However, my niece must continue her journey to her father's ranch, if she's to see him before he dies. That's where you come in. I want you to see that she arrives there safely.'

'Me?' Jack Danner yelped, his surprise total.

'That's what I said,' Spencer Bonnington snapped. Danner's gaze went to the driver and another man in Bonnington's employ, the snake-eyed gun-honcho who had been covering Bonnington from inside the stage when he had arrived in town. 'I'll need Ben and Frank to travel with me,' he said, guessing Danner's thoughts.

'Seems to me that your niece's safety should be your prime concern, Mr Bonnington,' Jack Danner said.

'There's no question that it is!' Bonnington flung back. 'When I board the train at Hanley, Ben and Frank will clip it back and meet up with you at Pointer Wells. The three of you will go on from there to my brother's ranch.'

'Why?' Danner questioned.

'What do you mean?' Bonnington asked.

'Well, why would I need to go on from Pointer Wells? I'm sure that these squarely built fellas will be more than up to escorting your niece from there.'

'I'd prefer three to two. Simple as that,' Bonnington said.

'That don't make sense, Mr Bonnington,' Danner stated.

'Is that so?' Bonnington said huffily.

'There's pretty rough country between here and Pointer Wells,' Danner said. 'With the risk of pretty rough fellas to go with it. After that, most of the rough riding and danger is done with. And if you're entrusting your niece to my care as far as Pointer Wells, I can't see no reason why I couldn't finish the journey on my own.'

Spencer Bonnington's answer was blunt.

'I'm a very rich man, Danner. There's a distinct possibility that I could be kidnapped and held for ransom. If that were not the case, then I would have no hesitation at all in having the three of you escort my niece from here.'

'Ain't it likely that your niece could suffer the same fate — being a Bonnington an' all?'

'Sarah does not have any wealth in her own right until she reaches the age of twenty-seven, Danner. That'll be five years from now.'

Danner's brow furrowed.

'I'm not sure I get the point. Kidnapping your niece would be pretty much the same as kidnapping you.'

'I won't have any truck with kidnappers, Danner,' Spencer Bonnington stated unequivocally. 'I've given the strictest instructions that were I to be kidnapped, not a dime is to be paid for my release.' His face hardened. 'And that goes for Sarah, too. I wouldn't pay a plugged nickel.'

'Kind of hard-hearted, if you ask me,' was Jack Danner's opinion.

'I'm not asking you, Danner,' Bonnington stated bluntly, and added, 'A thousand dollars. That's what your services to me are worth.'

Danner was dumbfounded.

'Interested?'

Interested! Bonnington's offer had almost stopped Jack Danner's heart.

'That's a lot of dollars, Mr Bonnington.'

'Every job has its price,' Bonnington said. He looked Danner squarely in the eye. 'Didn't think you'd hesitate at getting your hands on a thousand dollars, Danner.'

'The truth of it is, that I'm kinda intrigued, Mr Bonnington.'

'Intrigued?'

'Yes, sir. Ya see, I've been pretty much a foot-loose wanderer.' He grinned. 'I prefer that description to drifter or saddlebum. So I can't figure why you'd want to entrust your niece's care to me. I mean, ain't you 'fraid that once I get your dollars in my pocket that I'll take off and leave your niece at the mercy of whoever happens along, if the desert don't get her first.'

Spencer Bonnington grinned.

'Because, Danner, you won't see a dime of the thousand dollars until I get word that my niece has arrived safely at her father's ranch.'

'Sensible,' was Danner's response.

'And,' Bonnington went on, 'if anything happens to Sarah, I'll have you hunted down and your innards ripped out to feed to the buzzards.' Bonnington's features set in stone. 'The same will apply if you lay a finger on her.

'Now, all that's to be decided is how much do you want that thousand dollars, Danner?'

★　★　★

'That, Uncle Spencer, is the most ridiculous idea I've ever heard!' was Sarah Bonnington's fiery opinion the next morning at sun-up, when Bonnington told her that he had hired

Danner to be her escort. 'I wouldn't cross the main street with Mr Danner.'

'You'll do as I say, Sarah!' Bonnington barked. 'I am your guardian.'

'How can you just hand me over to . . . to . . . ?' Her green eyes looked contemptuously at Jack Danner. 'Words fail me!'

Jack Danner stood up from the chair he'd been sitting on in the hotel foyer and strolled to the door.

'Where are you going?' Spencer Bonnington demanded to know.

'Well,' Danner drawled, 'I reckon that eating grass would be preferable to a thousand dollars for nursemaiding your brat of a niece, Bonnington.'

'A thousand dollars,' Sarah Bonnington exclaimed, and swung about to face her uncle. 'You're paying this saddle-tramp a thousand dollars to escort me? Have you taken leave of your senses, Uncle Spencer? He'll just take your money and run out.'

'Don't you worry about that. Danner and I have a certain arrangement.'

'Brat!' Sarah Bonnington fumed. She picked up the hotel register and threw it at Danner. Danner ducked, and it went straight through the glass panels of the hotel door. Ben, the stage driver, grabbed her wrist as she tried to grab his sixgun.

'Stop it this instant, Sarah,' Spencer Bonnington commanded. 'Now, you are continuing on to your father's ranch and Mr Danner is going to see that you get there safely. Understood?' He turned his attention to Jack Danner. 'Isn't that so, Danner?'

Aware that he had Bonnington over a barrel, Danner made a show of hesitation.

'Fifteen hundred,' Bonnington offered.

'You have gone mad, Uncle Spencer!' Sarah Bonnington raged.

'I'm ready to head out whenever the lady is,' Danner replied.

'This cannot be happening,' Sarah exclaimed. 'I'm sure that your business back in Boston is not that urgent.'

'It's most urgent, Sarah,' Bonnington

said. He took his niece's hands in his. 'Can you for one moment think that had I a choice, that I would not see you to the end of your journey? Have I not always been kind to you?'

'Of course you have, Uncle Spencer. Always.'

'Then do as I want now, Sarah. Ben and Frank will meet up with you and Danner at Pointer Wells.'

'Aren't there Indians around here?' Sarah said fretfully.

'Apaches,' Danner said. Obviously aware of the Apaches' fierce reputation, Sarah Bonnington paled. 'Only they ain't no trouble no more. 'Cept of course if some white man don't go and kill an Indian. Then all hell'll break loose.'

'But I'm a white woman. Don't the Apaches — '

'There's no worse black-hearted critters than Indians when it comes to women, white, red or black. Those gents ain't pa'ticular.'

Spencer Bonnington glared at Jack Danner.

Danner shrugged. 'Best if she knows all the facts, Bonnington,' he said. 'That way I won't have to listen to her caterwaulin', if things go wrong.'

'Nothing will go wrong!' Bonnington barked. He turned to Sarah. 'A couple of days and you'll be with your father, Sarah. Isn't that what you want? You know that Nathaniel hasn't much time left.'

Tears flooded Sarah Bonnington's green eyes.

'Yes, Uncle Spencer. That's what I want. Don't you want to see him too?' Sarah asked her uncle.

'Of course I do. I'll head right back when I've finished my business, Sarah. Now, at all times, you be guided by what Mr Danner says. OK?'

Sarah Bonnington nodded.

'Good girl. Ben.'

'Sir.'

'Go to the livery and get two of the best horses the keeper has.' He took from his pocket a roll of dollar bills and handed it over to the stage driver.

'Time is of the essence. Don't haggle. Pay what he asks.'

'That'll be four horses,' Danner said. 'Two spare. That way we can change mounts and always have fresh horses at the ready, if we need them.'

Ben looked to Spencer Bonnington for directions.

'Good idea. Four it will be,' Bonnington confirmed. 'I'm sure Mr Danner knows his business.'

'Can't we use the stagecoach?' Sarah enquired.

'It would attract too much attention,' Danner said. 'And in the desert that's the last thing we need. Better to look poor. That way a man's passage is safer. Envious eyes can put a bullet in your back.'

'I hate riding,' Sarah Bonnington proclaimed. 'And horses don't like me.'

'Nags can get real ornery if they reckon you don't want their company, Miss Bonnington,' Jack Danner said.

'Well, I'm sure they'll soon learn manners when a good whip is laid on them!' she flung back. Danner, his eyes blazing, looked at Sarah Bonnington with utter contempt. 'You mistreat your horse when I'm around and I'll leave you high and dry in the desert!' he warned her. 'Understood?'

'Uncle,' she pleaded, 'are you going to allow this . . . this person to talk to me like that?'

'Your safe delivery to your father is what matters most, Sarah,' he said. 'And you'll have to do exactly as Mr Danner says.'

Sarah Bonnington's shock and surprise that her uncle had, for once, stood up to her, was total; so overwhelming in fact that the words that came to her lips could not be spoken.

'I'll get the horses,' Ben said.

'I'll get the horses,' Danner countered. The stage driver looked to his employer for guidance. 'If I have to ride it, I'll pick it,' Danner added, his attitude uncompromising. 'And I do the choosing on my own.'

'Give Danner the roll of bills, Ben,'

Spencer Bonnington ordered.

The stage driver handed over the roll of bills, but obviously thought that Bonnington had taken leave of his senses.

A half-hour later, Danner was back with the horses and ready to ride, until he saw Sarah Bonnington come from the hotel in skirts and looking like she had just stepped out of a fashion-store window.

'Look, Miss Bonnington,' he growled, by now his patience with the uppity young woman wearing thin, 'this is not some fancy show you're riding in. We'll be in the desert, a lot of the time on foot when the terrain gets too draining for the horses. So I figure that jeans would be more appropriate garb.'

'Jeans!' she yelped. 'I don't have any jeans in my wardrobe, Mr Danner.'

'Then mosey 'long to the general store and get some,' was Jack Danner's solution.

'I will remind you, that I am not some ragamuffin cowgirl, Mr Danner!' she fumed.

'No, ma'am,' he agreed. 'And that's the problem.'

Sarah Bonnington's green eyes flashed at her uncle, but on seeing his unwillingness to indulge her, she flounced off in the direction of the general store.

A little while later, Sarah Bonnington suitably attired and still fuming, Jack Danner rode out of Haley Ridge. Three days at most, he'd be $1500 richer, and Danner figured that with that sizeable a poke he might just forsake his wandering ways and join his brother in farming in Utah, if Sam Danner would have him around the place. Chalk and cheese, were the Danner brothers. Sam, the family man and church-goer, straight and honest in his dealings; Jack, the footloose philanderer, who had never taken a wife because he liked variety too much. And the last time he'd seen the inside of a church was when he had sought sanctuary from a trio of fast-drawing hardcases down Mexico way. Three days he had held out, protected by the Franciscan monks of the mission, feeling not the least shamed by what some would see as his cowardice, but what he saw as good sense. He had reasoned that one gun against three were odds that only an idiot would take. Being Mex bandits and ardent Catholics, they would not desecrate the church. After three days the hardcases tired of waiting and rode on.

'Those men will not give up on their revenge,' one of the monks cautioned Danner on his leaving the mission.

He didn't figure they would. But in open country, he'd stand a lot better chance of outwitting them. The next day the bandits showed themselves, but their timing was lousy. A bounty hunter, looking for a murderous cut-throat who had sought safe refuge in Mexico, alerted by the gunfire Danner was exchanging with the Mexican hardcases, pitched in on the side of a fellow-American. Being a pragmatic cuss, and in the bounty-hunter's debt, in return for his assistance in seeing off the Mex bandits, Danner pointed him in the direction of Seth Holt, the cut-throat he was hunting.

Riding at a steady pace, Danner again took to dreaming about returning to his brother's farm and putting down roots. It surprised him that he was thinking that way; he never had before, his only longing being to see what was on the other side of the hill. Maybe he should have taken up Sam Danner's offer of sharing the farm with him when their pa had passed on fifteen years previously. However, Pa had left the place lock, stock and barrel to Sam, the younger brother and his favourite, because for one reason or another the old man and Jack had locked horns almost from the cradle, and by the time he was ready to cast off the mortal coil, they were about as far apart as the walls of the Grand Canyon.

'You're welcome to half the land and half the house, Jack,' Sam had told him, after their pa had been lowered into his grave.

Jack Danner had thanked his brother for his more than generous offer.

'That's not the way the old man wanted things to be, Sam,' he'd said. 'He saw fit to leave everything to you and nothing to me.'

'Pa is gone, Jack,' Sam Danner said. 'I own the farm now. So it's my decision to share it with you.'

Jack Danner swung into the saddle on that cold and grey winter's day. 'Wouldn't want for Pa to be spinning in his grave, Sam,' he'd said, and had ridden away, his pa's voice ringing in his ears. 'You'll never amount to anything but a footloose saddlebum, Jack,' had been his often voiced prediction.

In the years since, as he drifted from one town and one territory to the next, seeking he knew not what, Jack Danner had often thought that the old man's assessment of him had been a shrewd one. Maybe he'd have upped and left anyway, even if the old man had left him the farm. There was no way of knowing for sure. But there was one certainty: Luke Danner had chosen well in Sam. He had worked hard, and had built a farm to be proud of, doubling the acreage. Now and then, over the years, Jack had wandered back secretly, and had been full of admiration for what Sam Danner had achieved. Once, he had almost hailed his brother, but, penniless, had decided against doing so. If he ever returned, he'd want to ride in proud and independent. Fifteen hundred dollars wasn't a fortune, but it was a darn sight more than he'd had together in a long time. Maybe Sam's offer of sharing would no longer be on the table. But at least, with $1500 to brag about, he could ride on with some of his dignity intact.

But before he could even think about returning, he had a pesky, spoilt woman to deliver to her pa. It should be a relatively easy ride, times having got a lot more peaceful in recent years with

US marshals roaming about, and the Indians learning to be farmers rather than scalp-hunters. However, in Jack Danner's experience, it was when trouble seemed far off, that it jumped up and bit a fella on the ass.

5

'Keep up!'

Sarah Bonnington, trailing behind, glared at Jack Danner. 'Why don't you try falling back,' she said. 'Where I come from, it's customary for a man to wait for a lady. Of course that would be a gentleman!'

Danner turned in his saddle, looking here and there. Then, with a wry smile, declared, 'I don't see no lady, ma'am.' Sarah Bonnington fumed. 'This is sure as hell going to be a long journey,' he groaned.

'Not as long for you as it will be for me!' Sarah flung back.

Jack Danner stifled his laughter. He had met a lot of feisty women in his travels, but he reckoned that Sarah Bonnington might just turn out to be the feistiest of them all. He drew rein to let her draw level, but she hung back a dozen horse lengths.

'Close enough, Mr Danner?' she asked spiritedly. 'It is for me.'

The cool of the morning was fast diminishing, and being replaced by the muggy heat blowing off the desert, foretelling the searing torture that lay ahead. Another hour, two at the most, and he'd need to find shade until the sun's intensity began to wane later in the day. He'd long since been weathered by the hostile climates he had ridden through, from Yukon snow to Mexican heat, and his tolerance to the furnace conditions of the desert country would be greater than the woman's. She had the milky skin of the city dweller. She had probably spent most of her time indoors or in beauty saloons, daring only to go out in the mildest of weather. It worried Danner that the challenges of the hard ride to Largo, would prove too much for her.

'Sarah's a lot tougher than she looks,' had been Spencer Bonnington's reassurance, when Danner had raised the question of her endurance with him. 'Her father was rawhide tough, and deep down, she's a chip off the old block.'

Looking now at the quickly wilting Sarah Bonnington, her uncle's reassurance was ringing hollow in Jack Danner's ears. She looked fit to topple out of her saddle.

'You OK?' he asked. 'Want to hole up for a spell?'

'Don't you worry about me, Mr Danner,' Sarah said starchily, coming upright and ramrod straight in the saddle. 'I'm just fine.'

'Don't want you falling from your horse and breaking bones,' Danner said. 'So you tell me in good time if you're feeling weak, you hear?'

'I sincerely hope that this trip can be completed with the least talk possible,' she said, her chin jutting defiantly.

'Ya know,' Danner growled, 'I've nursed cows less ornerier than you!'

'That was because they probably felt a kinship with you, Mr Danner: I don't.'

'Goddamit. You're one lippy filly.'

Jack Danner swung his horse and, stiff-backed, rode on ahead. Sarah Bonnington smiled. She was not used to backchat from males; most men she knew in Boston were fawning fops, only too eager to be her lapdog and concede every argument and give way to all her whims. But Jack Danner was different. He was the kind of man who took no nonsense, and was not afraid to tell her exactly what he thought. It surprised her that only a couple of hours previously she would not have walked on the same side of the street with a hobo like Jack Danner, and now she found herself feeling companionable towards him. Not that she'd let him know that. Were she to even hint at a change of attitude, he'd be preening himself no end.

Jack Danner's thoughts were not dissimilar. He reckoned that behind the spoiled brat were the makings of a damn fine woman, if only she'd let that woman emerge. But, like Sarah Bonnington, he'd be damned to Hades before he'd give her an inkling of the way he was thinking.

'There's a creek a coupla miles west of here,' he called back, drawing rein at a fork in the road. 'We'll rest up there while the sun's at its meanest.'

'Not on my account,' she called back. 'But if a gentleman of your years needs to *hole up* — isn't that what you say to describe a respite? — by all means we'll . . . ' — her cocky smile raised Danner's hackles — '*hole up.*'

Jack Danner would have loved to have come up with a clever retort, but try as he might to find one, his head remained empty.

'Respite, my ass!' he growled, and turned west for Indian Creek.

It was only a couple of miles to the creek, but they were miles that made the difference between what was bearable and what was exhausting. And by the time they reached Indian Creek, Sarah was clinging to her saddlehorn and hoping that she would not make a fool of herself by toppling off her horse in a faint. She almost made it, but not quite, and it was Jack Danner's alertness that saved her from serious injury, when the world spun around her.

6

'Darn!' Danner groused, once he had helped her from the saddle and the world was righting itself again. 'Didn't I tell you to warn me if you were coming over funny, woman?'

Her blood running hot in her veins, Sarah Bonnington berated Danner. 'You unsympathetic bastard!'

Jack Danner grinned.

'Well,' he drawled, 'nothing like a little criticism to get a woman's blood up. It's about a half-mile to Indian Creek. Reckon you can make it?'

'I'll make it if it's the last thing I do,' she said.

'Ya know,' Danner said, mounting up, 'I just can't figger what it was that I did that was so darn wrong for punishment like this.'

'We can always return to Haley Ridge,' Sarah Bonnington suggested.

'There might just be someone there of a sweeter nature and not as rude as a horse breaking wind who would be willing to take fifteen hundred dollars to take me to my father's ranch.'

Jack Danner's grin went from ear to ear.

'But no way near as handsome,' he chuckled.

'Hah! Handsome! A mule's rear end would be more handsome than you!'

'That's what all the ladies say before they kinda get a hankering for me,' Danner said, riding on, his shoulders shaking with laughter.

Sarah Bonnington's fury was so potent that it took away the breath she needed to respond, even if she could think of a response. But, infuriatingly, she could not. At least not one caustic enough to put the arrogant Mr Danner back in his box. However, had she a view of Danner's face, she would have seen a face that had lines of worry drawn across it, and would have understood that his laughter and repartee were an act to hide his worry, and convey the image of a man without a care in the world, when, in fact, he had many.

The clatter of shale down from a ridge covered by stunted trees and scrub, moments before Sarah Bonnington almost toppled from her horse, would probably have gone unnoticed by a less knowledgeable and less alert man than Jack Danner. The shale might have been dislodged by an animal or the natural movement of the terrain, but he had also heard a sound, though faint, that told him that the shale had been loosened by a two-legged critter.

The sound was the jingle of a spur.

He'd have changed direction to try and lose the company he had picked up, but there was no point. Alone, he could have probably outridden or outfoxed his watchers, but with a woman along, and one whose riding skills were passable but not up to scratch for fast riding in dangerous terrain, he'd not have a hope of success.

The men had chosen not to show themselves, which could mean only one thing: they saw a prize for the taking. Materially, they had nothing worth stealing. But in the flesh there was a great deal on offer — Sarah Bonnington.

It was country filled with canyons, gullies, draws and high ridges, ideal hideout country. There were in fact several owlhoot roosts scattered about. And, added to that, Mexico was within easy reach. Therefore there was a constant drift of hardcases going and coming. It was a vast country, and if a man was lucky he could ride it without trouble. However, if a man's luck was out, his passage could be fraught and likely deadly. With a woman for company, his chances of survival, should he cross paths with the kind of black-hearted and soulless men riding the desert country trails, dropped right down to zero.

Jack Danner was beginning to think that $1500 might in no way be enough compensation for the grief that might be his before this trip was over. That was, of course, if the ride to Largo did in fact end in Largo.

His grave might very well be right here in the desert.

7

Indian Creek was an amazing green oasis in the middle of desolation. Many reasons had been put forward for the lush resting place, the saving of many a man when hope had almost vanished, but no one really cared why the creek was there, they were just glad that it was.

'What's troubling you, Mr Danner?'

Sarah Bonnington's unexpected question took him by surprise.

'Troubling me?' he hedged. He had obviously underestimated her shrewdness. Foolishly assuming that age and wisdom complemented each other.

'I'm not a fool,' Sarah said stiffly. 'So don't treat me as one.'

'How did you cotton on?' he asked, his curiosity genuine.

'Your gait,' she answered simply.

'My gait?'

'Yes. I learned early on to study a

man's gait. A woman has to do that to avoid trouble. In my experience, Mr Danner, no matter how a man tries to hide what's in his head, it shows right there between his shoulders.'

'Clever gal,' he complimented. 'And, ah . . . could we drop the Miss Bonnington, Mr Danner, lingo?'

'Sure, Jack,' she said pleasantly. 'Now are you going to tell me what interpretation you're putting on that handful of shale that clattered down from that ridge a while back?'

Though Sarah Bonnington was a young woman, barely more than a gal, she was showing the grit of an older woman.

'I reckon that we've become the subject of curiosity, Sarah.'

'We? You mean I have, don't you, Jack?'

'I figure. This is wild and raw country. Men are in the saddle for long stints. They get . . . ' Danner shifted uneasily in his saddle. 'Ya see . . . '

'They get woman fever, right?'

'How the heck are you so knowledgeable?' Danner grumbled.

'Aren't you glad that I am? Otherwise, you'd choke on the words you've been trying to get out.' She rode alongside him. 'So, Jack,' she said, 'how are you planning to keep me safe from these licentious curs.'

'Li — what?'

'These men of ill-repute?'

'Don't you talk any western lingo?' Danner complained.

'Howdy. That's about it, Jack. I'm a Boston girl. I've lived there for most of my life. Uncle Spencer sent me to the best of schools. Introduced me to Boston's finest.'

'Didn't he know that some day you might make tracks back West?'

'That was not in the plan of my future. It was my father's wish that I should live in civilized society. Marry well. Have two children and no more. Preferably a boy and a girl. Care for my very wealthy husband, and die in silk sheets.'

'I don't understand how a man could let his little girl go and not regret it.'

'Oh, you malign my father, Jack. His heart was broken. But I was a little girl, without a mother. What could he do?'

'Marry again and keep you under his roof,' Danner suggested.

'When my mother died, he swore that no woman would ever replace her, and he's upheld his oath. He's spent his entire life building the finest and biggest ranch in Largo. When Uncle Spencer and he arrived in this country from England, they came with the meagre remains of what had once been a substantial fortune, frittered away by a drunken lecher of a father. Spencer sought his fortune in business in Boston. My father, his in the West. Both men thought that the other was insane. But, happily, both have been succesful in making good the fortune which had been stolen from them.

'Uncle Spencer, had he remained in England, would be a lord.'

They had arrived at Indian Creek.

'What now?' Sarah Bonnington asked.

'We ride in as if we don't have a care

in the world,' Danner said.

'What if those men are waiting for us?'

For the first time, Danner detected a hint of apprehension in Sarah Bonnington's voice.

'It wouldn't be possible for them to reach the creek before us,' was Jack Danner's conclusion, delivered with a confidence he was far from feeling. His knowledge of the desert was good, but in his experience of life, one man's knowledge was, somewhere along the line, bested by another's. A man could ride the desert country for a lifetime and always come across some new trails and tracks. Knowing what he knew, he had taken the most direct route to Indian Creek. However, he had no doubt at all that there were other even more direct trails there.

'Jack,' Sarah Bonnington said, 'you're going to have to stop trying to hoodwink me.'

'Hoodwink you?' he said, his face a moon of innocence. 'What the heck are you gabbing about?'

'Is the trail we've just ridden the only trail to the creek?'

'Probably not,' he said, seeing no point in lying. Sarah Bonnington seemed to be able to get right inside his head and know what he was thinking before he thought it!

'So why are we brazenly riding in?'

'To make those critters think that we don't know they're around, of course.'

'What happens if they don't play your game, and pounce?'

'Then,' Jack Danner grumbled, 'we've got a real big problem, Sarah Bonnington. By the way, can you shoot?' he asked, hopefully.

'No. Oh, I know what end of the gun a bullet comes from. But hitting someone with that bullet is the difficulty.'

Jack Danner's shoulders slumped.

★   ★   ★

A half-hour had passed.

'Looks like we worried about nothing,' Sarah Bonnington said, sipping her third cup of coffee and hating each mouthful, her taste being for tea, a habit she had acquired in Boston.

'Maybe,' was Jack Danner's preoccupied response.

Sarah could be right, but he did not think so. It was more likely that their followers were exercising caution. The creek was well protected by trees and boulders, and an incoming rider could not see much of it until he was actually in it. He had worried that he might be ambushed when he had ridden in, and that would also be their followers' concern. They could also be waiting for them to ride out of the creek, because what applied to riding in, also applied to riding out. Danner had thought about a scouting mission, but leaving Sarah on her own, even for a brief period, was too much of a risk to take.

'You think that we're still in danger, Jack?' Danner hunched his shoulders by way of an answer. 'We can't remain here forever.'

'That might exactly be the way they'd

figure,' Danner said, dourly.

'So what are we going to do? Grow old together?'

Jack Danner thought: I could think of worse fates. He was about to decide on moving out when three dusty riders put in an appearance. The lead rider he knew. His name was Bob Rand. The other two, he did not know. But, riding with Rand, guaranteed that they were no good — in fact downright rotten!

Jack Danner glanced at the sixgun he had hidden in a hollow tree stump within arm's reach of where he was sitting with his back to a boulder.

'Howdy,' Rand greeted affably. He took off his hat to wipe sweat from his brow, a tumble of fair hair with not a speck of grey showing. 'Sure is hot.'

'The creek's got plenty of water,' Danner said.

Rand looked around at the creek as if seeing it for the first time, which Danner sincerely doubted. Rand had spent a great deal of time riding desert trails, making himself scarce after another bank robbery, or another rape, or murder.

'That coffee smells good,' Rand said. 'Mind sharing it with me and the boys?'

'There's plenty to go round,' Danner said.

Rand stepped down. 'Mighty neighbourly, friend.' He turned to Sarah. He tipped his forehead. 'Ma'am.'

Bob Rand was a good actor. If Danner did not know the kind of murdering bastard he was, he would be ready to believe that he was in the presence of a gentleman. However, the second rider to step down, a round-shouldered runt of a man, was not as proficient. Or maybe he figured that there was no need to hide his obvious desire for Sarah Bonnington. The third man had the swagger of a man too preoccupied with his own importance to be bothered about anything other than convincing everyone else of that importance. Danner noted the polished smoothness of the walnut butt of his sixgun; a smoothness which was evidence of the gun's regular use. The man's blue eyes had the coldness of the born killer.

'You folks going far?' Rand asked, pouring coffee that was thick with brewing, in the friendly way that a man who was concerned for their welfare might.

'Largo,' Sarah said, filling the silence that was created by Danner's lack of an answer to Rand's question; an intended lack of reply. Because Rand's curiosity was motivated by his need to know their itinerary. If things did not work out the way he wanted them to at the creek, he could always, knowing their plans, plot his next move.

'Ain't too far,' was Rand's response. 'Got kin in Largo?'

'My father,' Sarah informed him, much to Jack Danner's annoyance.

'Your pa, huh. Maybe I know him. I visit Largo on business a lot, ma'am.'

'Better drink that coffee while it's still anyway warm,' was Jack Danner's advice to Rand. 'If you don't, it'll taste like coyote's piss.'

Danner's hope that his intervention would curtail Sarah Bonnington's flow of information was dashed.

'Nathaniel Bonnington's my father.'

Bob Rand's bleak grey eyes popped. 'The owner of the biggest ranch in the territory?'

'Yes,' she said proudly. 'I believe that that is so, Mr . . . ?'

'Charles, ma'am. Dan Charles,' he lied, with the smoothness of a snake's belly.

Shit! Unknowingly, Sarah had now added ransom to rape. She had gone from shrewdness to stupidity in a flash. That's how good an actor Rand was.

'Do you know my father well, Mr Charles?' Sarah enquired.

He shook his head. 'Only by reputation, ma'am.'

'By reputation?'

'Yes. As a fair and honest man.'

'That's good to hear.'

'The truth always is,' Rand purred, snake oil dripping from his tongue. He looked at Sarah squarely. 'Didn't know

Mr Bonnington had a daughter. And certainly not one as fetching.'

Sarah Bonnington blushed. 'Why thank you, Mr Charles. But you see, I've been living with my Uncle Spencer in Boston since I was so high.'

'Spencer Bonnington,' Rand became thoughtful, in the way a man trying to place a name became. But Danner had already seen the flicker of excitement in Rand's eyes on hearing the name of Spencer Bonnington. 'Don't reckon I've heard of him, ma'am,' the outlaw leader lied.

If he had his loose mouth in Sarah Bonnington, Danner took comfort from Rand having her equal in Rand's swaggering sidekick.

'Ain't he one of Boston's richest men?' he said.

Sarah laughed. 'I hear tell that he's worth a dollar or two.'

Jack Danner could not believe his misfortune. Sarah Bonnington had lost complete control of her tongue. He jumped up.

'I guess it's about time we were making tracks, honey,' he said to Sarah. The familiarity flummoxed Sarah. 'That is if we're to join up with those men you're pa has sent to meet us.'

Rand's eyes flicked, his alarm showing for only a second.

'You folks are married?' the runtish man enquired, unable to hide his astonishment that a man, not particularly handsome, and at least fifteen years older than the woman, was her husband.

Danner drew Sarah Bonnington into his arms and kissed her.

'I'm a very lucky fella,' he crowed.

Stunned, Sarah was about to strike out, but Danner's squeeze on her waist alerted her to his need for her to play along with his crazy scheme. She returned his kiss.

'And I'm a very lucky woman, too.' Hugging Jack Danner, she whispered in his ear, 'What are you playing at?'

'Just hold your tongue and give me another wifely hug, as if you really cared.'

Sarah Bonnington smiled as if she had just been handed the keys to heaven, and did as Danner asked.

'Well, I guess we'd best be moseying along, honey,' Jack Danner said, with the tone of a man well pleased with his lot.

'Anything you say, darling,' Sarah said, matching Danner's mood in spades.

Danner had been trying to figure out how he might retrieve his sixgun from the hollow tree stump in which he had hidden it. At the time he had hidden the gun, it seemed a shrewd and clever move. However, now, in retrospect, it was the dumbest thing he could have done, because with his rifle in its saddle scabbard, and his .45 in a tree hollow, he was weaponless.

The walk to his horse, hitched to a nearby willow was only a dozen or so paces, but in country where death only took a second to visit, it was a long way to have to go.

'You're holster's empty, mister,' the

man full of his own importance observed. 'Ain't you got a gun?'

Damn!

'I'll be . . . ' Danner's hand dropped to his empty holster. 'Must have lost it somewhere,' he said. 'This old holster ain't up to much.'

'Losing your gun in lawless country like this, ain't wise,' Bob Rand commented. 'In fact, downright foolish.'

'Yeah,' the runt chuckled. 'A fella's liable to meet all sorts of no-goods in this neck 'o the woods. Ain't that so, partners?'

'Now, Lucky,' said the man with the constantly itchy trigger finger, his tone scoffing, 'there ain't no call to scare these fine folk with loose talk like that.'

'Gee, I'm plumb sorry,' the runt apologized insincerely. 'I've got this great idea though. Why don't we ride along with these decent folk. Kinda escort them, huh?'

His glance went to Rand, as did Jack Danner's. The air crackled with tension.

'Well, thank you, fine gents, for the offer,' Danner said, amiably, hoping to pre-empt Rand's decision. 'But me and my wife wouldn't want to impose on your kindness and generosity.' Rand's gaze settled on Danner. The outlaw's gaze told him that Rand knew exactly what he was up to. 'But, like I said, my pa-in-law's sent some men to meet us.'

Danner looked about vaguely.

'Heck, can't understand why they haven't arrived by now. Can you, honey?' Sarah Bonnington rolled her eyes in wonder.

'But I guess they can't be far off,' Danner said, with the lazy tone of a man at ease.

Though Rand was almost certain that Danner was bluffing, there was just a smidgen of a chance that he was not. During the exchanges, Danner had edged a little closer to his horse and the precious rifle in its saddle scabbard. However, should Rand's decision be to take what he wanted now, Jack Danner did not hold out much hope of making it to the rifle in time to give an account of himself, ineffective as that account would probably be.

'We could rest up a spell in Largo,' the runt suggested to Rand, his eyes stripping Sarah. 'Ya see, we've been on the trail for a spell. What d' ya say, Bertram?' he asked the third man of the trio.

A moment before, on hearing Bertram call the runt Lucky, Jack Danner's blood temperature had dropped, because he reckoned that he was facing Lucky Moreno, a man with killing in his blood since the cradle. Born bad, he had steadily got more and more evil. And now, on hearing Moreno address his sidekick as *Bertram*, his blood dropped right to zero, because he had heard that Bertram Oakwood, a man who was even more evil than Moreno, had killed two men for calling him Bert. He was known for insisting that his full name and not its abbreviated form be used.

In Rand, Moreno and Oakwood, Jack Danner knew that he was in the presence of three of Satan's arch disciples.

'Lucky's got a point, Bob,' Oakwood said.

Rand shot him a furious glance. But even before Rand's visual rebuke, Oakwood had realized his mistake. Rand had already introduced himself as *Dan* Charles. Danner pretended not to notice Oakwood's slip of the tongue. But how would Sarah Bonnington react? Danner knew that if she gave the merest hint of spotting Oakwood's mistake, Rand would act now rather than later. Of course, there was the risk that he might act anyway, not wanting to risk Danner's claim of help on the way proving to be true.

The next second would tell.

8

Jack Danner tensed his leg muscles, making ready to lunge for the rifle. Get it right and he might at least take one of the trio with him, the runt, he reckoned. Because, clearly, he was the man who was the most immediate danger to Sarah Bonnington. His lust for her was burning a hole in his gut. He might, should Rand decide on later rather than immediate action, act anyway. Mistime or misinterpret Rand's decision, and he would not stand a chance of putting up even the token resistance he was planning.

'We don't want to impose on these lovebirds, fellas,' Bob Rand said expansively. 'Heck, we'd only be in the way. Ain't that so, folks?'

Sarah snuggled up to Danner.

'That's very understanding, Mr Charles,' she said.

Mr Charles. Clever girl. Any doubt that Rand might have about Sarah having spotted Bertram Oakwood's mistake was swept aside by Sarah's casually innocent use of Rand's alias. Danner helped Sarah into the saddle and then strolled to his own horse.

'If you fellas are in Largo in the next week or so, be sure to look Sarah and me up.' He swung into the saddle. 'We'd sure like you to visit. Ain't that so, honey?'

'Sure is, darling,' Sarah beamed.

'Thank you,' Rand said affably. 'Me and the boys will keep that in mind.'

'Keep a steady pace!' Danner ordered Sarah, when, the aftershock of fear taking hold, she wanted to gallop out of the creek. 'We've got to show no suspicion. Turn and wave.'

Sarah did as Danner instructed.

Jack Danner knew that they were still not completely out of danger. Rand could still change his mind and put a bullet in his back. Or one of the others could take the initiative — especially Lucky Moreno. He'd be eaten up inside at losing the pleasure of having Sarah, and his mood would be a festering wound. Driven by the oldest urge in the book, he might just throw caution to the wind. And Danner also knew that the bickering would have already begun and might just persuade Rand, in the interests of unity among them, to reverse his decision of a moment ago.

As he reached the top of the rise leading up out of Indian Creek, Jack Danner wondered how much luck was left in a pot he'd been taking from for a long time now. Five minutes later, and clear of the creek, the tension began to flow out of Sarah Bonnington and tears flooded her eyes. The confident and worldly woman she had masqueraded as vanished, to reveal the vulnerable younger woman — the real Sarah Bonnington, still more girl than woman.

'Will you just look at me,' she croaked. 'Going all weepy. What must you be thinking, Jack?'

'That you're one hell of a gal, Sarah Bonnington,' he replied sincerely.

'Oh, don't say what you think I want to hear, Jack Danner. Say what you mean. Truly mean.'

Danner drew rein.

'That you're one hell of a gal, Sarah Bonnington,' he repeated.

They rode on in silence, each preoccupied with their own thoughts: she, thinking that she had completely misjudged Jack Danner; he, thinking that were he a younger man he might just press a claim to Miss Sarah Bonnington. However, Danner had other thoughts crowding his mind too; thoughts about Bob Rand's next move. Because, as sure as night followed day, they were not free of his and his partners' malignant attentions. Somewhere between here and Largo, they'd meet up with Rand and his sidekicks again. Probably as soon as Rand was certain that help coming to meet up with him and Sarah was the fiction it was.

And there was the night ahead.

'How far to Pointer Wells?' Sarah asked, suddenly.

Had she picked up on his tension? Or was she reading his gait again? Consciously, Danner relaxed his shoulders.

'Too late, Jack,' Sarah said.

'Late tomorrow afternoon,' he said.

'Everything going well,' she said.

He nodded. 'Everything going well, Sarah.'

'We haven't seen the last of those men, have we, Jack?' Danner thought about lying again, but doubted if he could fool Sarah. 'When they realize that you lied about my father sending riders to meet us.'

Jack Danner did not answer her question. There was no need to. Besides, he was watching the smoke puffing from the hills to the west of them; smoke he had not seen in a long time — Apache smoke!

He was not fluent in reading Indian smoke, but he had what might be called a working knowledge of smoke lingo. And it told of an Apache woman and her boy having been murdered by white men, and the need to revenge them by killing many white eyes.

Jack Danner reckoned that his troubles were only just beginning.

9

Who in tarnation had been loco enough to kill an Indian? Even the hardcases who would kill for the simple pleasure of killing, would not have been crazy enough to risk an Indian uprising. The memory of the time when a whiteman's passage through the territory was a lottery that a lot of men had lost, was not so distant a memory to have its ferocity forgotten. So why would anyone purposefully risk the terror of a renewal of Indian trouble?

'Is that Indian smoke?' Sarah Bonnington enquired of Danner, her curiosity laced with apprehension.

'It is,' Danner confirmed.

'Apache smoke?'

Now apprehension outweighed curiosity in her question.

'Probably,' Danner said.

'What does it mean? Can you read smoke?'

'A little,' Danner said evasively.

Sarah Bonnington studied him carefully. 'How little? Or maybe that should be how much?'

'There's nothing to worry about,' Danner said casually.

'My understanding is that there's always something to worry about in Apache smoke. What does it say? From the little you understand, of course,' she added, pointedly.

Danner made a pretence of studying the drifting smoke.

'Something about a meeting of Apache bigwigs.'

'You're lying, Jack!' Sarah Bonnington stated bluntly. 'Now tell me what that smoke is really saying.'

'Have you no trust, woman?' Jack Danner blustered.

'Not in a conniving, two-timing, double-crossing charlatan like you, Jack Danner!'

Danner grinned the charmer's grin

that had so often filled his bed on a cold night. 'Heck, you do think a lot of me, don't ya?' he said.

'The truth, Jack,' Sarah pressed, worry haunting her green eyes. 'I'd prefer to know than be surprised any day.'

'The smoke talks of an Indian woman and a boy who have been murdered by white men,' he said, resignedly.

'Murdered? Who'd be insane enough to start a massacre?'

'That's a question that's been exercising my mind since I saw the smoke,' Danner said. 'It makes no darn sense to me.'

'The only reason there could be, is that someone purposely set out to start an uprising by killing the woman and the boy,' Sarah Bonnington said, making a whole lot of sense, matching Danner's thoughts on the matter.

Sarah Bonnington held Jack Danner's gaze.

'We're in deeper trouble now, aren't we, Jack?' she asked sombrely.

'Well, maybe we'll get rid of Rand and his cut-throats. It's likely that on seeing the smoke, they'll bolt for Mexico.'

'What's between here and Pointer Wells?' she asked.

'Desert.'

'I don't mean the type of terrain. I'm asking about what we might encounter.'

'I know you are,' Danner said wearily. 'It's Apache country.'

'Is there another way?'

Danner shook his head. 'From now on any bush could hide an Indian, Sarah.'

'How about going back?'

Jack Danner shook his head again.

'Back or forward is pretty much a throw of the dice,' he stated. 'But if you've got a preference, I'm willing to listen.'

'Forward,' Sarah Bonnington said uneqivocally. 'As I understood from Uncle Spencer, my father hasn't got that much time left before Gabriel's horn blows.' She became reflective. 'I'll not deny that I never wanted to start out from Boston for this godforsaken land to begin with. But, as I journeyed, I found myself wanting more and more to complete the trip. I guess that coming home means more to me than I ever thought it would.'

She laughed sadly.

'Maybe I should have made the trip sooner and in happier circumstances. I suppose that, despite my years in Boston, my roots are still here, Jack.'

'Yeah. Once it gets in your blood it's hard to shake, ain't it?' he said. He looked to the distant purple hills. By now the great balls of smoke were gone and wisps only drifted skywards. 'Giddup, hoss,' he urged the mare, 'Pointer Wells is awaiting.'

As they rode on, Jack Danner did not bother to check on his back trail. If Rand and his no-good partners were tracking him, they were expert enough not to let themselves be seen. And if Apaches were monitoring his progress, he'd not see them until they wanted to be seen. So he saw no point in straining his neck.

He began to think again about that pot of luck he'd been dipping in more frequently of late, and he wondered if there was enough luck left for him to make it to Pointer Wells. And he dared not think beyond that, and the $1500 waiting should he make it to Largo; a bounty that would help him to settle, because, as the years grew longer and lonelier on the trail, he had begun to think more and more about the town he'd one day ride into and not leave again. Or the chill morning he would not wake from the perished sleep of the night before. Unknown. Dumped into an unmarked pauper's grave. Or left to be devoured in the wilderness. And he had tired of the rebellious streak in him that had set him on the course he'd chosen. In recent times, he had become deeply conscious of the looks of contempt he received from other men. A no-good drifter and saddletramp. A man not fit to associate with. A failure. It was hard for Jack Danner to admit that increasingly he craved to be accepted, to belong, to be befriended. And in the short time he had been in Sarah Bonnington's company, all those needs had become even more focused. In her, he was seeing the woman he might have married; the woman who would have given him strong sons and pretty daughters, and with whom he could have shared the fireside of an evening. He had begun to think that if he grabbed his chance this time, and used Spencer Bonnington's dollars sensibly, he might still attain what he desired more and more now. A home. Roots. Peace of soul and mind. And a heart that was owned by a good woman.

'We'll travel through the night, if you're up to it, Sarah,' he said. 'We'll use the other horses. That way, by sun-up, we'll have covered most of the distance to Pointer Wells.'

'Won't night travel be dangerous, Jack?'

'It'll have its risks,' he confirmed.

'But they're risks I'd prefer to take than again crossing paths with Bob Rand and his cohorts. Or even worse, Apaches.'

'I'll be guided by you, Jack,' Sarah Bonnington said.

He chuckled. 'Well now, you might just be getting sense in that pretty head of yours, Sarah Bonnington.'

'What will you do with that fifteen hundred dollars Uncle Spencer will give you?' she asked unexpectedly.

'Haven't rightly thought about that yet,' Danner lied, hesitating to tell her of the dreams he'd been dreaming, in case he tempted fate and those dreams were snatched away from him, should the gods hear of his daring to think that he could reverse his fortunes.

'You could use it to cease your wandering ways,' Sarah suggested.

'Now ain't that just like a woman,' Danner laughed. 'Always wanting to change a man's ways.'

'Well, Jack Danner,' she responded, 'I think that you're the kind of man who will only change when it's you yourself wants to do the changing.'

'Is that a compliment?'

'More a fact,' Sarah said.

'Then,' Danner said cockily, 'I figure that it's the darnest compliment I've ever been paid, Sarah, my darling.'

He rode on, feeling as smug as a flea on a well-fed dog's rump.

10

Night in the desert came quickly, paying no heed to the problems of wary and tired travellers. The tension of the long afternoon, every second of which could have pitched him and Sarah into mortal danger, had left Danner feeling drained and wanting nothing more than to break his ride for longer than it took to make coffee and help himself and Sarah to a plate of beans. He searched for the right spot to break his journey; someplace that would not show the light of the fire he would need to brew up. He found it in a hollow surrounded by boulders. However, though it was suitable for preparing their meagre meal, it came with the disadvantage of allowing a predator of the four or two-legged variety to creep up on them through the very rocks and boulders that would hide the light of their fire from prying eyes.

'Maybe we should just keep on going, Jack,' Sarah said, realizing in a glance the precariousness of their stopover.

It was a proposition to which Danner gave credible thought. However, weakened by hunger, added to tension and sleeplessness would, come morning, see them in poor shape to fight off any attack made on them. With any luck, by sun-up, they would be within reach of Pointer Wells and the safety of the town. He would try and persuade Sarah to wait over in Pointer Wells until the Indian trouble abated. But he knew that her new found resolve to complete the journey to Largo to be reunited with her stricken pa, would not be easily overcome, and she would become even more determined when they joined up with the Bonnington hirelings in Pointer Wells. The more he thought about it, the less sense it made to Jack Danner that Spencer Bonnington should risk his niece's safety by retaining the services of his men. But he supposed that men like Bonnington, full of their own importance, thought first of themselves and everyone else second. And, of course, the financier could not have known that some crazy coot would go and stir up Apache trouble.

'We need rest,' he said. 'The horses too.'

'But lighting a fire . . . ' Sarah fretted.

Over the last couple of hours Sarah Bonnington's apprehension had grown. Danner could understand how it had. She had probably heard the lurid stories of how white women had suffered at the hands of the Apache. However, Danner had known white men who were a whole lot worse than the Indians. And there were many white men who did the deed and blamed the Indians.

The meagre meal was over with in a short time, but, despite being edgy to go on, Danner rested up for an hour longer. With the need to constantly check every step, night travel could be even more draining than crossing the desert in the heat of the day, and Sarah Bonnington's lack of know-how in avoiding trouble was an extra worry he had to contend with. She was a skilled rider by Boston standards. However, riding through a Boston park, or galloping over the open soft pastures around the city, was a far cry from the rocky, often deceptively devious terrain she was now negotiating. Her unfamiliarity and inexperience with western terrain would be a drawback that would slow their progress to little more than an amble. And Jack Danner dared not contemplate what he would do if there was a need to make fast tracks. He wondered where Rand and his hardcase pals had got to every bit as much as to where the Apaches might be lurking, because he considered them at least enemies of equal threat. The Indians would go on a blood-letting rampage, and in that way their paths may or may not cross. Rand, on the other hand, would carefully plan and scheme to corner Sarah Bonnington and kill him. He was not worth a plugged nickel to anyone. But Sarah, now that Rand knew who she was, was a pot of gold for the taking by demanding a ransom from Spencer Bonnington for her release. Rand would never believe in a thousand years that it was Bonnington's avowed policy never to have any truck with kidnappers.

'Jack.' Danner put aside his morbid thoughts on hearing Sarah's soft call. 'Are we going to make it to Largo? Be honest with me now.'

'Truth is that I don't know, Sarah. But I'll do my darn best, that I promise you.'

'Funny, isn't it, how you find so many things you want to do, when you might not have the chance to do a thing,' she said soulfully. 'How life, that you didn't care much about a short time ago, suddenly becomes the most precious thing of all.'

Danner spilled the dregs of coffee on the dying fire.

'Let's make tracks,' he said.

11

Luck was running against them. An hour after setting off from the hollow, in which their progress had been trouble-free and reasonably quick, the full moon which had helped that progress became fickle and mean with its help, dodging behind straggles of cloud that pitched the desert into mineshaft darkness, and what had been negotiable terrain suddenly became unnavigable treachery. The landmarks that had stood out sharply in the moonlight were now ill-defined and in shadow as the cloud thickened. Jack Danner knew that guessing in the desert could have a man going round in circles or ending up where he least wanted to be. As the moon's hidden periods became longer, Danner was forced to dismount and walk the horses. And when it finally vanished behind a bank of impenetrable cloud, his progress was halted, probably for the best he reckoned, despite his keen frustration at having to hole up. His problem come first light would be that he would be in flat open country with, as he could see, only sparse cover and easily visible to watching eyes. He could only hope that come morning their exposure would not be as complete as it had appeared to be in the moon's final brief light.

'Might as well try and get some shut-eye,' he told Sarah.

'Sleep,' she scoffed, in a voice that had more than a little hysteria in it. 'And wake up scalped!'

Another time Danner might have pointed out the illogicality of her statement, but he figured that were they to laugh at it, which he hoped they would, that laughter would only come when they were safe in her pa's ranch house.

'You'll be safe enough from Indians

until sun-up,' he assured her.

'And Rand and his cut-throats?'

'They'll have holed up for the night, too,' Danner said.

His first assurance he felt pretty certain of. However, his second less so. With Indians on the prowl, Rand and his partners would also see the advantage in night travel. And there was also the possession of Sarah Bonnington and the eventual ransom they might get for her to drive them on.

'You think so, Jack?' Sarah asked worriedly.

'Surely do,' Danner lied.

Settled to a restless pretence of sleep, Danner's ear was cocked for the slightest sound or whisper. He wished that he had not had to leave his sixgun in the hollow of the tree back at Indian Creek, because the rifle he clutched under his blanket would be more difficult to manouevre than the smaller weapon should he have to act swiftly. Shortly before first light would be the most dangerous and more probable time for an attack, just when there was enough light to see by, but not enough to prevent a man drifting through the grey shadows between the fading night and coming day.

12

Morning came, calm and uneventful, blessed with a clear light that washed over the desert. In the distance, Danner figured a mile, two at most, no distance at all in desert terms, he saw smoke from a chimney curl up into the clear air. He could never reason why a man would want to farm or ranch in the desert, but there were some who preferred its challenge to the greener pastures on its rim. And, of course, there were those who had stopped right where they were when they had run out of grit to go on or their horses simply dropped.

'Do you know where we are, Jack?' Sarah Bonnington asked, looking about her in trepidation at the purple and orange vastness of the desert.

'On course for Pointer Wells,' he told her.

'How can you find your way out here?' she wanted to know.

'There's sign,' he said. 'Lots of sign. Get to read it, and it's like walking down a Boston street.' Jack Danner chuckled. 'In fact, I'd probably get lost a whole lot quicker on a Boston street than I would out here, Sarah.'

His laughter deepened. 'Firstly, I don't read so good, and all those street names wouldn't mean tiddly to me.'

'But you worked in Boston, didn't you? At Uncle Spencer's club?'

'Yeah. All of three weeks 'fore I got the urge to smell horse sweat and saddle grease again. Had a fancy notion that I'd take to city living.' He shook his head. 'Darnedest notion I ever got in my crazy skull.' He sighed deeply.

'When my time comes, I'd prefer to topple from my saddle and let that be an end of it.' He shook himself free of his reverie. 'Let's mount up and head for that curl of chimney smoke,' he said, pointing into the distance.

Sarah screwed up her eyes.

'I don't see any chimney smoke,' she said.

'Well, you wouldn't. You're looking with Boston eyes, Sarah. A coupla months, if you stay round that long, seeing that chimney smoke will be second nature.'

★　★　★

An hour later, during the second half of which Danner kept a steady eye on a cloud of dust to the south of him, not too distant to have the gap closed quickly once the tilt in the ground evened out and they became plainly visible where, Danner reckoned, the settler's abode would come into view. How much of a dash he'd have to make to its refuge, should he have to, worried him gnawingly. Pretty soon he'd have to alert and instruct Sarah, and it was not a burden he liked placing on her already heavily laden young shoulders. And it was a real pity that the dust could not tell him if it came from unshod or shod horses or ponies. Shod, might be troopers on the move. Unshod, Indians.

Shortly before the terrain evened out the dust cloud drifted away, indicating that the riders had drawn rein or changed direction, the latter he hoped. He decided to hold off on scaring Sarah more than she already was. Ten minutes later they arrived at the flat open stretch that led to a shack. The barren ground behind the creaking edifice had wilting, straggling crops clinging to soil that was more dust than earth, which marked the shack owner as a farmer. Danner checked his surroundings and saw no sign of anyone else. He eased the mare forward, tensed and ready to break in to an all-out gallop, if trouble suddenly reared its head.

Drawing nearer the shack, he saw a grave out back of it, a rotting wooden cross lolling sideways, desert foliage reclaiming the ground with the tenacity of the dispossessed.

'Quiet, isn't it?' Sarah murmured.

'By the look of decay and rot round here, the farmer's probably sleeping off one of a thousand skinfuls,' Danner joked.

But Sarah was right. It was quiet — too quiet. In fact utterly soundless. And in the desert there was always some sound, with its creatures of air and earth continously foraging and challenging for what little sustenance there was.

Jack Danner had expected a challenge to be offered to his progress towards the shack. Any sensible dweller would try and ascertain in good time if it was friend or foe approaching. His edginess grew as he came within rifle shot of the shack. Perhaps the owner was a shoot-first-ask-questions-later sort.

He drew rein.

'Be ready to turn tail and ride helter-skelter if needs be, Sarah,' he cautioned, and hailed, 'Hello the house! Mind if a coupla weary travellers come a-calling?'

There was no response. He thought

about increasing the volume of his summons, in the event that the shack-owner might be hard of hearing. But he was conscious of how sound travelled in the desert. Feeling naked to any watchers, he waited for as long as he could before he approached the shack, again drawing rein nearer the house, where he repeated his call to its occupier.

'If the farmer is drunk, he must be as close to death as doesn't matter,' Sarah said, trying for a lightness of tone that was overcome by worry.

'Stay here,' Danner instructed her. 'I'll check out the shack.'

'I'm not sitting pretty here,' Sarah Bonnington protested, joining Danner as he moved forward. There was no time for argument, his concentration on the shack needed to be absolute. As it happened, he rode right up to the shack without challenge.

'Wait here,' he told Sarah, dismounting. 'And don't argue,' he growled, when it seemed likely that she would again challenge his order.

He approached the shack, already knowing in the sound of buzzing flies, the reason for the stillness from within. He pushed open the door and the stench of blood wafted out of the shack. The farmer, the top of his head gone, lay sprawled across the table, flies nesting in swarms feeding on his brain. And to the side of the shack, against its wall, a woman lay slumped, only the skimpy remains of her blonde tresses covering her bloodied scalp. Her eyes were wide open, the images of her final agony stored in them.

The blood was fresh. Recently spilled. Which meant that there were probably Indians close by. He would have to forsake the rest and grub he had anticipated and move on quickly. How much more could Sarah Bonnington take? he wondered. Her scream told him that she had reached her limit. Jack Danner spun around just in time to grab her as she fainted.

13

Conscious of every second he remained in the open, Danner quickly got her inside the shack and, as Sarah stirred back to consciousness, he placed himself between her and the shack's bloody corpses. But even without visual stimuli, her brain provided instant images of the nightmare. 'Easy,' Danner counselled, as Sarah went to sit up abruptly and the shack spun round her. 'Just lie still for a minute. You'll be just fine.'

'Lie still?' she wailed. 'With the stench of fresh blood in my nostrils?'

She fought him, but he held her firm for a moment longer before letting her up. Immediately he had to grab her again when she tried to bolt outside.

'Let me go!' she berated Danner, clawing at him in her distress.

'I don't know who's out there,' he

told her. 'Be hasty and you might just end up like the folk here.' The starkness of his warning jolted Sarah Bonnington. 'Shut your eyes and hold your breath. I'll go outside and take a look-see.'

'You take care, Jack,' she fretted.

'Goes without saying,' he replied.

Easing open the shack door an inch at a time, he stepped outside. Sarah went to the window, careful to keep her back to the butchered dead, anxious to keep in visual contact with Danner. Her concentration on what was happening outside the shack made her oblivious to the danger within, and she did not notice the slowly opening trap door to the shack's roof space.

★　★　★

Danner's eyes scanned every inch of the terrain he could see, and saw nothing. It looked like the Indians had done their worst and ridden on to seek retribution elsewhere for the murder of the Indian woman and the boy. Satisfied that there was no threat from the terrain in front of the shack, he edged round to the rear of the shack. Thankfully, the country to that side was also devoid of threat. However, he knew that trouble and menace in the desert came swiftly, often materializing malignantly out of what appeared to be the most benign circumstances. With any luck, he'd reach Pointer Wells by nightfall. He prayed that he would not have to spend another night in the desert. If he had to, it might be the catalyst that would send Sarah Bonnington spinning into craziness.

* * *

Sarah craned her neck to watch, as Jack Danner went to the rear of the shack. The shack had no rear window from which she could watch, and she spent a fraught minute until Danner reappeared, smiling, and walking with an easy gait. Her relief was immense. Had her instincts not taken a battering, she would probably have been alerted to the Apache about to drop down from the roof, only feet behind her, gripping a blood-stained scalping knife.

Danner was strolling back to the shack when he saw through the window from which Sarah was looking out, the Apache behind her, about to reach out for her.

'Behind you, Sarah!' he shouted.

Sarah swung round. Immobilized by the fear of seeing the Indian, she stood stock still, rooted to the spot. The Apache buck was puzzled. He would have expected the woman to scream and flee. Was this white woman defying him? Well, he would soon teach her a lesson. He lunged at Sarah. She staggered back. Danner crashed through the rotten shack door. The Indian swung about. Danner grabbed a chair and flung it at him. He ducked under the flying chair and came up, knife poised and ready to gut Danner. Instinctively, Danner's hand dropped to his holster, only to find it empty. The Indian cleared the table in a single leap and landed toe to toe with Danner, knife slashing. Danner felt its bite on his left cheek. Blood spurted from the gash, and Danner knew that the loss of blood would quickly weaken him. If he was to successfully deal with the Apache, he had very little time in which to do so.

14

The Apache also knew the effect of his knife slash on Danner, but he did not want to wait for the white man to weaken from loss of blood. He was impatient to kill him, then the woman would be his. The Indian's frame of mind was what Danner had hoped it would be. The Apache's lunges were ungainly, hurried and easily dodged. Danner had his eye on the pistol lying on the table near the dead farmer's hand, where it had slipped from his grasp. His plan was to draw the Indian closer to the weapon, and hope that he would not, in his anxiety to kill him, realize until it was too late the danger the pistol posed. Of course, that was if the gun had bullets.

Worryingly for Jack Danner, the Apache seemed to calm himself and become more thoughtful about his wild attempts to nail him.

Through the haze of her terror, Sarah Bonnington knew that, defenceless as she was, she would have to try and do something to help Danner. The knife slash on his cheek was pouring blood. It would have to be stopped soon. Shock and rapid loss of blood would quickly debilitate Danner. Up to now the Indian's urge to possess her had driven him and he had taken risks which, had Danner a gun, would have seen the Apache dispatched to Hades. However, that lack of weaponry had forced Jack Danner to dodge and bide his time until he could find a niche in the Indian's guard that would allow him to get past the Apache's slashing knife. But, the shack being a small structure, he was fast running out of dancing room. Another cut and that would end it for Danner, and the beginning of her descent into terror.

The flicker of Danner's eyes alerted Sarah to the gun on the table. Throwing caution to the wind, she dived for the sixgun. Danner would have prefered had she tried to divert the Apache's attention, and given him the chance to reach the pistol. It would be a miracle if she reached the gun, let alone fired a shot.

Attracted by Sarah's movement, the Indian spun round, seeing in an instant the purpose of her dive for the table. He tried to upend the table, but the weight of the beefy dead man lying on it held it down. It had all happened in a flash, but it was enough time for Danner to wade in. His boot caught the buck in the ribcage just under his heart, but the Indian soaked up the punishment. Aware of how the odds had shifted, he opted to grab Sarah by the hair and used her as a shield against Danner's onslaught. For a second his hold on Sarah seemed firm, but her silken hair slipped through the Apache's clutching fingers and she broke free of his grasp. However, her weight, added to the Indian's as they crashed against the table sent it spinning. The gun flew across the floor to the far corner of the shack, and more out of reach to Danner than it had previously been. A bottle of rotgut on the table slid off and smashed on the ground. In the shattered bottle, Danner saw a weapon as deadly as the Apache's knife. He snatched from the floor a long, curved section of glass and rammed it into the Indian's throat. The severed jugular gushed blood. The Indian reeled back, pressing his fingers to the ragged wound, trying desperately to stem the tide of blood pouring from it. Hatred as raw as the ugly wound in his throat drove him to one final effort to kill the white man. He came at Danner in a crazy, loping stride that almost caught him by surprise, and might very well have done so, had Sarah not shoved the Indian to send him off balance. He collided with the shack wall behind Danner, his knife slicing into his belly in a final irony.

Sarah ran to Danner's arms, shivering like the last fall leaf on a tree. He let her cry herself out. It was best to let her drain herself of the emotions of the terrible ordeal that the hard ride to Largo had become.

'Will you just look at me,' she finally said, wiping away her tears. 'Caterwauling while you bleed like a pig. I'll get something to stop the bleeding.'

'There's only one thing that will stop this fast,' he said. 'Burning.'

'Burning!'

'Yes. Get some kindling and start a fire. Then clean the Indian's knife and heat its blade.'

'You can't be serious,' Sarah questioned, astonished and repulsed by Danner's instructions.

'We can't wait around here while I nurse this wound. And, truthfully, I won't be around if I don't stop this bleeding. So do as I say. Quickly, Sarah,' he urged her, when the awful spell of what he intended held her fast.

A short while later, Sarah watched with horrific fascination when Danner cauterized the wound with the heated knife blade. She swallowed hard and swayed when the burned flesh puckered, and its awful smell filled her nostrils.

'If there's anyone going to faint around here it'll be me,' he joked, gritting his teeth to bear the searing pain.

As he slumped back against the wall, Sarah came to comfort him, desperately trying not to breathe in the stench of his scorched flesh.

'A coupla months from now I'll be as handsome as I've ever been,' he told her, continuing with the humorous tone he had set a moment before.

She joined in.

'You know, Jack,' she said, looking sideways at Danner, 'I think that you never looked more handsome. That scar will sure give your face an intriguing aspect that should bring the ladies flocking.'

'Yeah,' he chuckled. 'Mebbe I should do the same to the other cheek.'

'Well, that would be cruel. A woman can only take so much handsomeness.'

Sarah wiped the sweat from Danner's forehead and brushed back his dark fringe. 'You've certainly earned Uncle Spencer's dollars, Jack,' she said softly.

He stood up shakily. 'We've got to get out of here, Sarah,' he said.

'You're in no fit condition to travel,' she said, concernedly.

Jack Danner gritted his teeth against the pain.

'I sure don't want to wait around here permanently,' he said. 'There could be another buck or two trailing the main party.'

The fear in Sarah Bonnington's eyes was instantaneous.

'Lean on me,' she said. 'If you fold, I'm done for.'

'Fold?' He grinned. 'We've got a date with your pa in Largo, Sarah Bonnington, and I'll be damned if I'm going to miss it. So get this old man in the saddle and we'll ride.'

'You're not old, Jack,' she murmured, her eyes clashing with his, flashing a message that flattered Danner. But it was a message he could not afford to respond to, because he had nothing to offer Sarah Bonnington other than grief. He was a drifter and would probably die a drifter. Besides, when the danger of the desert was over and they were safe in Largo, Sarah's eyes would be opened wide and she would again see him for what he was — a saddletramp, the man she had, only the day before, despised.

'Too old, Sarah,' he said with a soft regret. 'Worse darn luck.'

Sarah Bonnington's regret at his rejection hurt her keenly, and he almost changed his mind. But his resolve held. With hindsight she would understand the kindness and wisdom of his rejection, and hopefully he would ride away a friend. The fact was that not in his wildest dreams could he have hoped that a woman of Sarah Bonnington's quality and class, would feel kindly towards him.

Spencer Bonnington's dollars would mean a great deal to him. But, on setting out, would he have ever thought that they would come in a very poor second best to Sarah Bonnington's approval?

Setting out from the shack, Jack Danner was full of feelings he had never suspected he had, and he began to dream again of going back to his brother's farm; quitting the endless trails he'd been riding; sitting by a log fire of an evening; lying in a feather bed instead of the rocky ground his back had become used to; being useful and of good standing; not being shunned.

He was still dreaming when, riding through a draw, Bob Rand blocked their progress.

15

'Easy, mister,' he warned Danner, as he stiffened in his saddle. Bertram Oakwood appeared at the top of the draw to his left, Lucky Moreno, to his right. 'Now we don't want no trouble, friend. And there won't be any, if you'll hand over the woman.' He sneered. 'Ya didn't think we believed that cock-and-bull yarn about you and her being man and wife, did ya?'

Oakwood and Moreno joined in Rand's cruel and mocking laughter.

'Shove your nose up your ass, Rand!' Danner growled. 'The woman stays with me.'

Bob Rand's disbelief was genuine, and it took him a while to respond.

'You'll die,' he said.

'Every man's got to go sometime,' Jack Danner said. 'But I reckon that I'll have you for company, Rand. 'Cause if it's the last thing I do, I'll kill you.'

'Brave words for a man who's not packin' a gun,' Rand said. He pulled Danner's sixgun from inside the belt of his trousers. 'Found it in that hollow tree stump you hid it in back at Indian Creek. Not so clever a move, as it's turned out.'

'I've got a rifle,' Danner said, with a calm that he was far from feeling.

'You'll never reach it.'

The threat was Oakwood's, itching to drop him out of the saddle then and there, and have no further argument about it.

Jack Danner fixed his gaze on Rand.

'You want to gamble on that, Rand?' he asked.

'Just give the word, Bob,' Moreno growled.

Rand was shaking his head in wonder. 'You'd die for the woman?'

'I will,' Danner replied without hesitation.

'That ain't smart, fella,' Moreno said. 'We'll have the woman after you're dead, anyway.'

'You do, and I'll rise up and rip your throat out, Moreno!' Danner barked.

But Moreno had spoken a lot of sense. Danner got to thinking about changing track from his brash stance.

'Heh,' Oakwood mocked. 'I think we've got us a man in love, partners.'

'Love!' Moreno yelped, obviously not understanding the concept. 'Women's for takin', not for mollycoddlin'.'

'You know, I've changed my mind,' Danner said.

'Figured you would,' Rand sneered.

'I'll kill the woman first,' Danner said. Bob Rand sat bolt upright in the saddle. 'That way, we all lose.' Danner could sense Sarah Bonnington's shock, and he wished he could send her a glance of reassurance. But he had to make Rand believe that he'd do as he said. 'If I let you have the woman you'll kill me anyway. So I aim to deprive you of the woman.'

'He's bluffin', boss,' Moreno said.

'Then call it, you lump of coyote shit!' Danner barked. 'That's the only way you're going to find out, ain't it?'

Moreno and Oakwood looked to Rand for direction.

'I agree with Lucky,' Oakwood said. 'The bastard's bluffin'.'

Jack Danner laughed. 'A real dilemma, ain't it, Rand? Are you ready to risk all that lovely money you've been dreaming of squeezing out of Spencer Bonnington?'

'To hell with the money!' Moreno snapped, the fever of lust on him.

'Shuddup!' Rand growled. 'I'm tryin' to think!'

'What's to think about?' Bertram Oakwood asked, ready to challenge Rand's authority. 'He'll never reach that rifle in time.'

Bob Rand seemed about to be persuaded by Oakwood's argument.

'But what if I do?' Jack Danner said, pitching Rand back in to indecision.

It was a daring and dangerous game he was playing. And Jack Danner knew that it was a game that could go horribly wrong in a flash. Rand had become jumpy. And a jumpy man could, in the blink of an eye, become a deadly foolish man.

'Of course, there is one other way to play this,' Danner said, another plan springing to mind.

'Yeah?' Rand was ready and eager to listen. 'What way would that be?'

'I was thinking we could become partners.'

Jack Danner let his glance include Oakwood and Moreno.

'Partners?' Rand asked suspiciously, obviously stunned by this turn of events.

'We could make the ransom for this fine filly a four-way split.'

Danner looked at Sarah, desperately trying to flash her a message, but at the same time careful not to alert Rand and his buddies to the long term purpose of his bargaining. Sarah looked back at him with stunned contempt. He could only take the consolation that her reaction was an indication of how successful he was being as the villain of the piece.

'Forget it!' Oakwood snarled.

'Now hold on, Bertram,' Lucky Moreno said, grabbing the chance to be near to Sarah Bonnington. 'This is a three-man outfit, remember? We should vote.'

Oakwood sneered. 'Still got the hots for the woman, eh, Lucky? Well, the way I figure it, once we get our mitts on Spencer Bonnington's dollars, we can have a whole bevy of women to do anything we want with.'

'I'm still boss of this outfit,' Rand reminded his partners.

'Outfits change bosses all the time, Bob,' Oakwood said, with quiet menace.

'Are you aimin' to try and change the boss of this outfit, Oakwood?' Rand growled.

Jack Danner was growing more hopeful by the second that the trio would solve his dilemma for him by killing each other.

Oakwood gave long consideration to his reply.

'I guess not right now,' he said.

'Well, any time you're ready,' Rand barked. 'You just feel free to try!'

'I'll keep it in mind,' Oakwood scoffed.

'I say we become a foursome,' was Lucky Moreno's opinion.

'A four-way split, huh?' Rand questioned Danner.

'Fair, I'd say,' Jack Danner responded. 'After all, I'm providing the goods for ransom.'

'I ain't givin' you a plugged nickel, mister,' was Oakwood's stance. He addressed his next comments to Bob Rand. 'I take my share. You can divide the rest the way you please.'

'It's still a good deal, Bob,' Lucky Moreno pressed on Rand, unable to keep his eyes off Sarah Bonnington. 'I'll give every cent of my take just to have that lady's company for a spell.' He switched his gaze to Danner. 'You don't have no objection, d'ya?'

Jack Danner shrugged indifferently. 'Spencer Bonnington's paying me fifteen hundred dollars to escort his niece to her pa's ranch in Largo. Now, if I can up that fifteen hundred to a coupla thousand and maybe a whole lot more . . . ' He shrugged again.

Bob Rand snorted. 'You ain't no better than us, friend.'

'Never said I was, Rand,' Danner replied.

Sarah Bonnington came alongside Jack Danner and slapped his face as hard as she could, which was, Danner thought, hard enough.

'Guess you two ain't friends no more,' Moreno sniggered.

Danner rubbed his jaw.

'Guess not, Lucky,' he said.

'I like a woman I have to tame,' Moreno said, leering at Sarah.

'Come near me and I'll kill!' she swore.

'You're goin' to know what it's like to be used, Miss high-and-mighty,' Moreno snarled.

'My uncle's men will skin you alive once we reach Pointer Wells,' Sarah predicted.

Jack Danner winced. He'd be damned if that woman could keep her mouth shut. She had already spouted off about who she was back at Indian Creek and put herself in the way of being kidnapped for ransom. And now she had to go and tell these hardcases about the men who would be waiting in Pointer Wells; men whose help Danner was counting on to make it to Largo.

'I reckon we've spent enough time jawing,' Danner said. 'Are you fellas forgetting that Apaches are on the prowl looking for scalps? Already got a couple at a shack a ways back. I figure we should eat up desert.'

His hope was that he could cover up Sarah's loose talk, but he had no such luck. Rand pounced on her mistake with the rapidity of a buzzard on a tasty morsel.

'Men at Pointer Wells?' he asked, his eyes mere slits.

'Two fancy dans, no problem,' Danner chuckled.

'That's right,' Rand said. 'They won't be. 'Cause we ain't goin' no way near Pointer Wells. I know a hill trail that'll take us right to Largo.'

'That might not be wise,' Danner counselled. 'If we don't turn up at Pointer Wells, Spencer Bonnington will come looking.'

'That's a chance we'll have to take Mr . . . ?'

'Danner. Jack Danner.'

'Danner,' Rand concluded.

'Please yourself,' Danner told Rand. 'So long as you know that Bonnington has the dinero to raise a long-riding, fast-shooting posse.'

Rand was cocky. 'No one's goin' to be loco enough to join a posse with Indians on the warpath.'

'Dollars in a man's hand can make him real foolish,' Danner cautioned. 'Ain't much for a man to do in Pointer Wells since that mine closed. Mouths to feed.'

Rand was unmoved or unconvinced.

'We take the hill trail,' he stated unequivocally.

Lucky Moreno expressed his doubts about the wisdom of Rand's decision.

'The hills will be full of those damn savages.'

'Ridin' 'cross open country to Pointer Wells is ev'ry bit as risky,' Rand growled.

'In open country a man can see what's comin',' Bertram Oakwood pointed out.

'Yeah, it's true that a man can see trouble comin', but if you see, you can also be seen. We take the hill trail to Largo,' he said with finality. 'Let's move out.'

A sidewinder slid past in the sandy earth. And by the look Sarah Bonnington was giving him, Jack Danner reckoned that she'd prefer the sidewinder's company to his. It grieved him that he had to appear to throw his lot in with Rand and his no-goods. But couldn't Sarah see that, alone, he didn't stand a chance. And neither did she. He could not risk telling her of his plan to wheedle his way into Rand's confidence, and then grab any opportunity to turn the tables that might come his way. Maybe, he hoped, that when Sarah's reason cleared, she would cotton on to what he had in mind.

Before then, he hoped that she did not get her hands on a gun.

16

'Ain't we headed in the wrong direction?' Danner quizzed Rand, when the outlaw leader began to back-track. 'Largo's due south. We're heading east.'

'There's a canyon we can cut through to pick up the hill trail a coupla miles back. That way we'll give Pointer Wells as wide a berth as possible.'

'Canyons are risky in Indian trouble,' Danner warned.

Rand shrugged. 'Ev'rywhere's got its draw-backs with Apaches on the prowl.'

That was a fact.

'Kind of round 'bout way, if you ask me,' was Danner's opinion.

'I ain't askin',' Rand barked.

During the next couple of hours they saw several dust clouds and were forced to hole up, dangerously lengthening their journey. The Indians were obviously present in ever greater numbers, as smoke rose from the hills to co-ordinate the Apache raiders. They came across two more slaughters, a wagon with a man, a woman and two children butchered, and an old-timer, a prospector by the tools of his trade strapped to his mule, his belly slit open.

Bertram Oakwood was the first to put the point of view that they should seek the shelter of Pointer Wells, the nearer destination, until the Indian uprising would be put down.

'We go on to Largo,' Rand declared stubbornly.

'Money ain't much good to a dead man,' Oakwood argued.

'We've ridden through Indian trouble before,' Rand reminded Oakwood.

Continuing his argument, Oakwood groused, 'You're pushing luck that could run out at any second.'

The outlaw leader angrily drew rein.

'You want out, Oakwood?' he flared. 'You're always free to ride your own trail.'

Jack Danner saw a flash of raw hatred

in Oakwood's narrowed grey eyes, and was caught between hoping that the hardcase would throw down the gauntlet to Rand, and fearing that if he did the ensuing gunplay would probably have every Indian for miles around headed their way. In the desert sound travelled far and wide and twisted and curved, making it difficult to pinpoint its location. But Indians, used to the accoustic vagaries of the desert, and with ears attuned to the terrain's peculiarities, would have no such difficulty. They'd come swarming, and if that happened the likelihood of them making it out of the hills were as close to nil as did not matter. Any intervention by him to ease the tense situation, which had become more tense during the sullen, ill-tempered ride since Oakwood had challenged Rand's authority back at the draw could, due to his newcomer status, serve to worsen rather than better matters: either man could interpret his intervention as backing for his opponent. Therefore, he welcomed Lucky Moreno's attempt to ease the bad blood between Rand and Oakwood.

'We gotta stick together,' he said. 'At least 'til we're outa this neck o' the woods,' he urged his partners.

Rand was the first to see the sense of Moreno's advice.

'Lucky's right,' he stated. 'Gunfire will bring Apaches crawlin' all over us.'

'Sure it will, Bertram,' Moreno said, when Oakwood was less ready to listen to his plea. 'Ya don't want a coupla hundred 'Pache bucks vyin' for your hair, d'ya?'

In a bloody-minded mood and looking for some return to salve his bad-temper, and also to annoy Moreno, Oakwood suggested, 'Maybe we should cut the woman loose all together. Indians will pick up the scent of a white woman from miles away.'

Now the ill-will that had been between Rand and Oakwood switched to manifest itself between Oakwood and Moreno.

'The woman stays!' Moreno barked.

'You'd risk your scalp to bed her?' Oakwood scoffed, and taunted, 'You've sure got it bad, Lucky.'

Taking advantage of the heated exchanges between the outlaws, Jack Danner let his hand drift towards the rifle in its saddle scabbard, weighing up his chances of the rifle clearing leather should hostilities break out. If gunfire started, then it wouldn't matter a damn, and he might as well try his luck in reducing the odds against him.

Behind him, Sarah Bonnington observed the cautious drift of Danner's hand towards the rifle and wondered if, by alerting Rand to Danner's intentions, she might curry enough favour with the outlaw leader to save her from Lucky Moreno's obvious intentions towards her. Danner had, to her surprise and shock, thrown in his lot with the outlaws, so she owed him no loyalty. But why was he readying himself to draw his rifle? Would it not have been

151

better not to take sides and remain neutral? In the absence of a threat to him, what had he to gain by becoming involved in the dispute?

Sarah Bonnington did not have a clear-cut answer, but she did have a notion that stopped her from taking the action she was contemplating.

Danner saw that Oakwood's sniggering remark to Moreno shifted the threat of gunplay from between him and Rand to Moreno and Oakwood. He glanced with alarm at Sarah Bonnington's position in the small clearing they were in. Unwittingly, she was directly in the line of fire between Oakwood and Moreno. If shooting started, there would be little chance that the flying lead would miss her.

'Ya know, you're a real pain in the rear end, Oakwood,' Jack Danner said, shifting position to in front of Sarah.

Bertram Oakwood's angry eyes flashed at Danner. 'That a fact,' he growled. The tension in the group had shifted again. 'I take your opinion as a real insult, Danner.'

'I don't give a damn, Oakwood!' Danner flung back.

Oakwood's anger went up several notches.

'Let's see if your draw is as fast as your mouth, mister,' the hardcase challenged.

'I'm not packing,' Danner said.

Bob Rand, relishing the chance to rid himself of the interloper, took Danner's sixgun from his saddle bag and tossed it to him.

'Now you have,' the outlaw leader said.

The look of concern in Sarah Bonnington's eyes pleased Jack Danner. Maybe it was her own welfare she was worried about, but somehow he flattered himself that it was not entirely so. Danner grabbed the gun sailing through the air.

'You're a dead man, Danner,' Lucky Moreno chuckled, the trio's disputes now forgotten in the common cause of getting rid of him, and having Sarah

Bonnington all to themselves.

'Tell you what, Moreno,' Jack Danner intoned, 'when I kill Oakwood, you're next.'

'Kill Bertram?' Moreno laughed. 'He's the fastest I seen.'

His laughter heightened, but it had an edgy uncertainty. Danner was an unknown quantity. And sometimes, but not often, a killer like Bertram Oakwood fell to an unknown gun.

Oakwood had no such doubts.

'You call it, Danner,' he said, his confidence sky high.

Jack Danner's first instinct was to keep on riding when he had visited Haley Ridge, but he had been sucked into a game of blackjack. Now, facing one of the fastest guns around, he knew that, as previously, he should have trusted his instincts.

'I'm waitin', Danner,' Bertram Oakwood growled.

Danner wondered how long Oakwood would wait? A year or two might not be too long, he mused.

Sarah Bonnington was not privy to how fast a draw Jack Danner had, or Oakwood for that matter. But she had a sinking feeling that Danner had bitten off a whole lot more than he could chew, and that puzzled her. One minute he was pitching her to the wolves, and the next minute he was risking his very life going up against an out-and-out killer like Oakwood. The man made no sense. Why had he stepped in to get Moreno off the hook, and put himself in mortal danger? He could have simply sat back and let them kill each other. In fact, if they had, he'd have an even split of any ransom with Rand.

She was still reeling from Danner's betrayal and treachery, so why she should worry if Jack Danner died or not was a mystery to her. But she did worry.

'Draw, or I'll cut you down,' Oakwood warned.

Danner had tried to buy time in the hope of fate coming to his rescue. However, it seemed his luck, on which he'd drawn liberally of late, had run out. In the split-second his hand went for his gun, his thoughts were of Sarah Bonnington and what now lay in store for her, and of how he had failed to protect her. In fact, he had played several wrong hands which had only compounded her plight.

Oakwood's gun was clear of leather a full second before his, and that was way too much time.

Sarah screamed, diverting Oakwood's attention. The second had been regained. Both guns blasted together, but Oakwood's shot went harmlessly skywards. Danner's bullet caught Oakwood on the left shoulder. But it was the arrow in his back that had killed him. The Apache Sarah had seen higher up in the rocks was joined by two more. Quick as lightning going to ground, Jack Danner leapt from his saddle and took Sarah with him to the ground as arrows rained down, one of which bit the dust inches from Danner.

'Stay there,' he ordered Sarah,

shoving her between a pair of high boulders overhung by a narrow ledge.

His previous dilemma had been reversed. Back at Indian Creek he had only a rifle when he needed a sixgun. Now he had only a sixgun when he needed a rifle. Shooting at the Indians high up, was purely for effect. He'd have to have the devil's own luck to hit one of the trio. Thankfully, Rand and Moreno, used to sudden action in their line of work, had found cover and were laying lead on the Indians, one of whom toppled from his perch. The other Indians ducked. They'd have time to wait. The gunfire would bring help. To reach them, the two men with rifles would have to make it across the clearing to the cover of the rocks below to begin their climb upwards. It would be a foolish risk to take. On the other hand, the white man who had taken cover at the foot of the rocks could work his way upwards.

Bob Rand saw the same risks and

possibilities that the cunning Apaches saw.

'Try and work your way up to within shootin' range, Danner,' Rand shouted. 'Lucky and me will cover you.'

The outlaw leader's strategy made a lot of sense. Danner's position made it impossible for the Apaches to nail him without standing up to aim directly downwards, which would make their position mighty perilous. However, from Danner's point of view, Rand's plan did have one major flaw, and that was that a couple of moments before Rand and Moreno were willing to let Oakwood kill him. What guarantee had he, should his mission to outmanouevre the Indians be successful, that they would not then add him to Oakwood and the dead Indians. High up, with only a sixgun by way of response to any threat, he'd be a sitting target.

'What're you waitin' for, Danner?' Rand bawled, as another shower of arrows forced him and Moreno to take

cover. 'Those bucks might have partners with rifles nearby.'

If they had, with all the lead slinging,
they'd be making fast tracks.

'Toss me your sixgun, Rand,' Danner
demanded.

'What for? You've got your own.'

'It's not for me. It's for the woman.'

'Why? She probably wouldn't hit the
side of a barn from close up.'

'I want the gun so that if you fellas
come eye to eye, she can kill you.'

'I'm not stupid enough to let the golden
goose be killed off, Danner,' Rand said.

'I'm not sure that you're that clever,
Rand,' Danner replied. 'Just now you
were about to indulge gunplay with
Indians on the prowl. If I don't come
back down out of the rocks, you might
be just as stupid again.

'Or maybe that hole-in-the-head
partner of yours might . . . Well, let's
say become over anxious, and blow
your brains out to have the woman.'

Bob Rand shot a furtive glance
Moreno's way.

'You ain't gonna listen to him, are ya, Bob?' Moreno whined. 'We're partners.'

His response was to toss Danner his sixgun.

'Ya know, Danner, I reckon you're soft on the woman yourself. And all that we're-in-this-together shit was to buy time.'

'Is that so, Jack?' Sarah asked.

'Take it,' he shoved the sixgun at Sarah. 'I've got no time now to talk.' He called back to Rand, 'Make that cover fire real good, Rand.'

As he went to break cover, Sarah grabbed his arm. 'Answer me, damn you, Jack Danner,' she demanded of him.

'Yes,' he admitted. 'I had to play for time, Sarah.'

Sarah Bonnington's next question was asked in a soft whisper. 'And is Rand right about you being soft on me, Jack?'

'You're just a gal, Sarah.'

'Woman,' she said. 'I started out as a girl, but I've become a woman, Jack.'

'What's keepin' ya, Danner?' Rand

demanded to know.

'Keep your hair on,' Danner called back.

'That ain't funny, Danner!' Rand growled.

'Come back safe, Jack,' Sarah said, as Danner broke cover and began to climb up through the rocks.

The Indians began an excited chatter. Danner hoped that it was because of his attempt to get close to them, and not because they had seen other Apaches approaching. Lead peppered the rocks, some bullets not as far ahead of him as Danner would have wished. He was only too aware that a stray or a ricochet could be as fatal as any intentional shot.

One of the bucks defied the odds and leaped down into the rocks above Danner. From where Sarah was, she could see that Danner was unsighted. The Indian had vanished from sight, and was probably lying in ambush for Danner.

Her heart began to race faster than it had ever raced before during her dangerous journey, because she now saw Jack Danner as her future. Who could have made her believe that when she so reluctantly set out from Boston, she would never want to return. She had fallen in love, both with the country and Jack Danner. And as things stood, it looked like her dreams were not to be fulfilled.

Should she call out to Danner? Or trust to his guile to outwit and overcome the Apache. The Indian was little more than a boy, but muscular and agile, and no doubt cunning as a fox. The decision was made for her when the Indian rounded a boulder and came up behind Danner.

'Behind you, Jack!'

Sarah Bonnington's desperate scream rattled through the rocks. Danner spun round. But with the Apache already leaping through the air, tomahawk ready to open Jack Danner's skull, had she left her warning too late?

17

With the suddenness of his turn, Danner slipped on a patch of shale and he fell sideways. At first he cursed his luck, because his ill-fortune would put him at a disadvantage. Then, seconds later, as the Apache buck shot past and crashed to the hard, stony ground beyond him, Danner realized that his slide on the shale had been good and not bad fortune. He sprang up and was on his feet, sixgun cocked, when the Indian came upright. Understanding fully the turn of fortune which had favoured the white man, the buck was left with no alternative but to charge straight at Danner in the hope that he would reach him before he fired his pistol.

Though not a man to use a gun if parleying could solve the problem, Jack Danner knew that this was not a time for hesitation. The Indian took the full blast of the sixgun in the chest, only inches away from Danner, so swift had he been. His momentum took him forward on top of Danner and he fell backwards.

The second Indian leaped into the rocks; the outlaws' guns remained silent. Sarah watched in horror as the second buck dispensed with caution and came right at Danner who was pinned under the Apache's dead comrade.

'Shoot, damn you!' Sarah screamed at Lucky Moreno, whose position to nail the maurauding Indian was more advantageous than Bob Rand's was.

'Why?' he sneered. 'Looks like them 'Paches are goin' to solve a problem, don't it?'

Sarah turned to Rand. His sneer matched Moreno's.

Danner fired, but only managed to slow the Apache rather than stop him, and the side wound only served to hike the Indian's anger and determination.

Danner threw off the dead Indian and rolled behind a boulder. He was on his belly when the Indian leapt on the boulder above Danner, figuring that Danner would not have time to roll on to his back and shoot, his triumphal, savage scream echoed in the distance.

Sarah fired her sixgun. But the shot went high and wide. She had only one other weapon which had to be of more use than the pistol, and that was herself. She sprang from cover, whorishly tearing open her blouse and fanning out her long blonde hair.

Her cavorting diverted the Apache's attention for only a sliver of time, but it was enough for Danner to nail him, blasting most of his face away. Sarah Bonnington's yelps of delighted relief filled the air. However her elation was cut short by the report of Moreno's rifle as he shot Rand in the back. His second buzzed close to Danner.

'You stay right where you are, Danner!' Moreno ordered. 'Me and the lady is leavin'. Get on your nag,' he told

Sarah. And when she hesitated, threatened, 'If'n you don't right now, I'll drop Danner.'

Knowing the hopelessness of his situation, with only a sixgun to respond to Moreno's rifle, which he could obviously use with expertise, Jack Danner bitterly instructed Sarah Bonnington, 'Do as he says.'

'Real sensible advice, woman,' Moreno crowed. He fired, and Danner's hat flew off his head. 'The next one goes right 'tween his eyes,' he told Sarah.

'You'll kill him anyway,' Sarah reacted fiercely.

'Mebbe,' Moreno laughed evilly. 'But, ya know, I figure I'll leave him for those 'Pache boys to find. It'll sure give me pleasant nights, dreamin 'bout what they did to him.'

'Go on, Sarah,' Danner said. 'I'll catch you up. That I promise.'

Sarah reluctantly mounted up.

'I don't think so,' Moreno said, in reply to Jack Danner's promise. He took possession of Danner's water canteen. Then he took Rand and Oakwood's horses in tow, and shot Danner's. 'Just in case them 'Paches don't git ya,' he chuckled.

'I'll come looking, Moreno,' he promised grimly.

'Ya know, woman, I figure that fright has completely unhinged Danner's mind,' Lucky Moreno told Sarah Bonnington. 'Giddup, horse!'

Helpless, Danner watched them ride away. Moreno had overlooked one important detail — the Apaches' ponies. Once Moreno and Sarah were out of sight, Danner hurried up through the rocks, praying that on the other side he'd find the ponies, and that the gunfire had not spooked them. On reaching the summit, he was relieved to see three ponies patiently awaiting their riders' return. He went down the other side of the rise with featherlike steps. The ponies were becoming restless, picking up the unfamiliar scent of the man approaching them.

'Easy now,' Danner coaxed the pony nearest to him, whose ears were twitching and nostrils flaring. 'This little ole white man means you no harm.'

The pony backed away.

The second pony, further away, picking up on the first pony's nervousness became even more agitated. If one of the ponies bolted, the others would follow suit, and he'd be left as Moreno intended, stranded, facing the slow death that the Apaches would inflict on him. Or the equally painful slide into oblivion that the desert would inflict.

The pony nearest backed off some more. Danner stood perfectly still, deciding that his best plan would be to let the ponies get used to his presence, in the hope that familiarity would bring trust. But that would take a long time, time wasted which would open up a wide gap between him and Moreno. There was also a breeze picking up, and that breeze would scatter any sign left by the outlaw and Sarah in the sandy soil.

How long could he afford to be patient? That was the question uppermost in Jack Danner's mind.

18

Slowly, the ponies became less and less restless in his presence. Danner knew that timing and instinct were all important in approaching. If he mistimed, the ponies' fears would rush back and they'd take fright. He grabbed a fist of rough desert grass and walked slowly towards the ponies with his offering held out for one of them to take. The pony he had earlier planned on grabbing shifted uneasily and moved away. But at least he had not galloped off. Danner gently held out the grass to the second pony, who remained sullenly steadfast for a few moments before he cautiously approached Danner to take the grass. Tempted, Danner almost grabbed the pony. However, he resisted the urge, reckoning that a little further time spent on building a bond of trust was better than blowing all the patient work he had already put in. But he was acutely aware that every minute spent in waiting, could be the minute that would make the difference between life and death, were more Indians to turn up.

He sat down carefully and waited to let the pony make the next move. After about half an hour, the pony came closer to him, and then over the next half-hour or so began to nudge him. Getting up slowly, Danner drew the pony to him with the rope reins. Danner got another fist of grass. The other ponies watched suspiciously. Danner knew that any anxiety communicated by him would be disastrous.

Feeling that he'd done all he could do, and had been as patient as he had time to be, Jack Danner mounted the pony.

'Easy, fella,' he murmured, rubbing the pony's mane gently. 'You and me are friends, right?' The pony shifted uneasily, knowing that the rider on him was not its usual master. Unused to a trousered rider, he hunched his back against the feel of the cloth. 'Easy.' Danner coaxed the pony. Slowly, over breath-stopping seconds, the pony settled down. 'Now, we've got some territory to cover, friend,' Danner told the pony. 'So when you're ready, I'm ready.'

There were more heart-stopping seconds before the pony made tracks. A second pony followed on. Danner saw this as a welcome bonus. Two ponies were better than one. The second pony was not yet ready to accept him, but by the time he needed to switch mounts, Jack Danner was hoping that he would be.

He checked his pocket watch. Two hours had passed since Moreno had kidnapped Sarah Bonnington. It was a lot of time to make up. And in the last half-hour, the breeze had become a wind and Moreno and Sarah's sign would be blown every which way. All he could hope for was sign that the wind would not affect. The tell-tale sign of a broken twig or a hoof scrape on a rock.

Horse droppings too could give a tracker an idea of when the man he was tracking had passed that way. And also, if analysed, could point to a white or Indian rider by the ingredients of the droppings. Though with the long treks through the desert that men like Moreno were forced to make, the oats that a white-man's nag would normally have in horse droppings, to distinguish it from an Indian pony, would not be present as the horse's diet would more or less match that of an Indian one.

In the end, he'd need a mountain of luck to catch up with Lucky Moreno, because each false trail would see the outlaw widen the gap between them. Perhaps the outlaw would continue with the gang's plan to ransom Sarah, in which case he'd head for Largo. On the other hand, Moreno's desire for Sarah being so driven, the ransom might very well be of secondary interest and he could head for Mexico, where he could trade Sarah when he tired of her. Or he could seek refuge in one of the roosts scattered about the desert, where, were he of a mind to, he could strike the same bargain for Sarah as he could in Mexico. And the third option open to the outlaw, would be to simply ride deeper into the desert and enjoy Sarah longterm. All of which stuck in Jack Danner's craw.

The $1500 Spencer Bonnington had agreed for Sarah's safe delivery to her pa's ranch in Largo, no longer mattered. Given the choice now, Jack Danner would have gladly traded Spencer's bounty for a mere glimpse of Sarah Bonnington.

★ ★ ★

Most of the day had gone and the purple of evening was spreading across the desert when, at a low point, Danner saw the strands of long blonde hair stuck in a bush. Of course the hairs could belong to another woman who had passed that way, but Danner reckoned not. Sarah was cleverly leaving sign for him to follow.

Danner picked up the strands of hair and felt them. They were fresh, not dried by the sun and wind. That meant that they had been placed there by Sarah recently — very recently. Jack Danner's elation was quickly followed by frustration. Darkness would come swiftly now. He had seen the strands of hair purely by chance. However, in the darkness there would be no hope of picking up further sign, if Sarah had had the chance to plant it.

Danner glanced to the sky, and the storm-heads rolling up from the south. Desert storms were unpredictable and fickle. It might hit him head on or veer away, there was no way of telling. But if it came, it would come in a deluge; a downpour that would obliterate any sign Sarah had left. He decided to go on, and use the little light that was left. If he waited, and the storm broke, the sign would be lost.

★ ★ ★

175

An hour later, night well established, Jack Danner was regretting his decision to proceed, because now he reckoned that in country with myriad gullies, draw and canyons, he'd have to backtrack at first light to be sure that he had not missed anything.

Time wasted.

He was about to swing into a hollow to camp for the night, when a glint of firelight further along the twisting trail caught his eye, a sudden leap of flame, possibly as firewood collapsed. It was a fleeting glimpse of another presence, but in the darkness finding whoever it was might not be easy. He wished for a moon. But the problem with that was that he would be seen as well as see. It might be Moreno and Sarah. But it might also be Indians.

He dismounted and made his way forward on foot, hoping for another show of light to direct him, but none came. He paused to ponder, and that's when he heard Lucky Moreno's voice.

'You'll catch a chill sittin' way over

there, Miss high-and-mighty,' he said. 'Now if you won't come over here, then I'll have to come over there.'

'I'll kill you if you come near!'

Sarah Bonnington's voice. Strong and forceful. Jack Danner's heart did a crazy little jig.

'Big words for a woman 'lone in the desert,' Moreno snarled, and then added mockingly, 'You've got poor ole Lucky shiverin' in his boots.'

Danner heard the jingle of spurs: Moreno on the move.

'You stay away from me!' Sarah warned. But her fiery resolve of a moment ago was gone, replaced by raw fear.

Danner would have liked to move more quickly, but in the desert stillness movement had to be measured and prudent. If Moreno got a hint of his presence, he'd undoubtedly use Sarah as a bargaining chip to save his scruffy hide. However, when he heard the unmistakable sound of material ripping, caution was no longer an option. He sprang into the outlaw camp.

Moreno spun round, as agile and quick as a rattler's fang.

'Well, ain't this a surprise,' he said. 'I thought the 'Paches would be roastin' you over a fire by now, Danner.'

Seeing Sarah draw her torn blouse around her, Danner's anger knew no limits. He charged Moreno. Surprised by the audacity of his action, the outlaw was caught off guard as Danner sank his head in his belly. Arms around the outlaw's hips, he drove Moreno back. They crashed to the ground. Moreno athletically tossed Danner to come out on top. He grabbed a rock and slammed it down where Danner's head should have been, had he not rolled aside. Moreno grabbed Danner's leg, but Danner broke the outlaw's hold with a punishing back kick that caught Moreno in the chest. The outlaw cried out, but quickly absorbed his pain. A knife flashed in Lucky Moreno's hand. Danner went for his sixgun, but found an empty holster. The damn gun was never where it should be when he needed it most. A gun blasted. The knife leaving Moreno's hand lost its momentum and went wild of its target. He turned to face Sarah Bonnington, clutching at his back where her bullet had made a sizeable hole.

'I told you I'd kill you if you came near me,' she said, and fired again.

Lucky Moreno's guts spewed out through the gaping hole in his belly. He fell dead, his surprise frozen on his face.

Sarah began to tremble violently. Danner took her in his arms.

'I killed a man,' she wept.

'You killed something evil,' Jack Danner corrected. 'Something that needed killing.'

She clung to Danner, her body shaking. He held her until she calmed, and he then told her, 'You sleep. I'll keep watch. First light we'll move on.' He grinned and tipped up her chin. 'By this time tomorrow, you'll be with your pa in Largo.'

Sarah Bonnington returned his grin.

'You know, Jack Danner. I believe we will.'

19

Despite her protestations that she could not sleep, exhausted as she was by the tension of her journey, Sarah quickly fell into a deep slumber, leaving Jack Danner alone to ponder. His thoughts were dark and dreary, adding further weight to shoulders already heavily burdened. The ride to Largo could still have many obstacles to overcome, but at least he could take consolation in knowing that the Rand outfit was no longer a threat. Sarah stirred a couple of times, her face reflecting the terror of her dreams. And towards morning, she mumbled words that momentarily elated Danner. 'I love you, Jack.' But then sent him spiralling into depression at the impossibility of pursuing any union with the woman who was fourteen years his junior, and pure as the driven snow, whereas, his past was chequered, and most times nothing to take pride in or comfort from, riding trails that went nowhere and sleeping wherever he could lay his head under the stars, or sometimes, if he was lucky, in a livery loft or a farm outhouse. Then he grinned, although somewhat sadly, when he thought that the man in Sarah Bonnington's dream might be some well-heeled Boston tyro. After all, Jack was not an uncommon name.

As the first streaks of dawn lightened the sky to the east, he woke Sarah to partake of the meagre breakfast of coffee and biscuits he had prepared.

'Easy, Sarah,' he said softly, as she came from sleep suddenly, eyes wild, her mind obviously full of the terror she had had to endure. 'We'd better make tracks.'

'How far is Pointer Wells?' she asked, nibbling on an unappetizing biscuit.

'We're not going to Pointer Wells. We'd have to backtrack. Don't see any point in doing that, Sarah,' he explained.

'But there's help waiting in Pointer Wells, Jack. Help we could very well need before we reach Largo,' she pointed out.

It was hard to argue against her reasoning. However, Danner's instincts were telling him to follow Bob Rand's plan to reach Largo by the hill trails. There were many to choose from, some barely passable, others decidedly dangerous due to the wear and tear of desert storms that washed out whole trails, alternating with heat that turned earth to a fine dust unable to hold rocks and boulders in place. Dislodged they came crashing down to block passage, or, if a traveller was unlucky, flatten him under their onslaught.

The threat of storm from the previous evening had not materalized, but Danner could see that the storm-heads were still in evidence. Though distant, once they picked up momentum from the desert heat, riding on the air currents, they could sweep up on them very quickly or not bother them at all. If the storm came their way, the hill trails would become conduits for water pouring down from higher up, and many would be converted to raging rivers. He did not consider the Apaches. Danner saw no point: there was no way he could plan for their appearance. In reality, as far as the storm went, the same applied to fickle nature. He'd prefer to have lingered awhile to see if the storm decided on a definite course, but the fact was that the storm could keep him guessing for hours.

'Our luck can't last forever, Jack,' Sarah said. 'And we've been riding it fairly hard. I think we should make for Pointer Wells.'

'I know what you say makes sense, Sarah,' Danner conceded. 'But I've just got this gut feeling that we shouldn't go anywhere near Pointer Wells.'

'Gut feeling?' she wailed.

'Out here, most times, that's all a man's got,' Danner said, and added with finality, 'We head for Largo.'

Overruled, Sarah became a sullen partner. Being of a feisty nature, she would not take being dictated to well.

He had known Sarah for only a short time, but Jack Danner had seen enough to know that she had in her the grit it took for a woman to succeed in the West. And as she learned, that grit would become all the more pronounced. The Sarah Bonnington who had ridden out of Haley Ridge had vanished. And in her place the woman who would be Sarah in the years ahead had been born.

Soon after breaking camp, Danner got the feeling of being watched.

★　★　★

Before heading into the steeper hills, Danner made for a water-hole which he had not visited for some time to replenish almost empty canteens. He hoped its water would still be good. Often in the desert, a man's luck ran out at a water-hole the water of which had become fouled by nature, or tainted on purpose. The Apaches knew the value of water as a weapon.

Partaking of bad water could be a death sentence. Leave it, and the end result could be the same. It was a dilemma he hoped he would not have to face.

The heat had been relentlessly building. By mid-morning, it had the blast of a furnace. And it could only get worse as noon approached. The storm still hovered, but he could tell from the heat-shrouded horizon, it had not made any move in their direction.

'Maybe we should draw rein for a spell,' he said, on observing Sarah Bonnington's wan lethargy.

'We'll go on,' she said, forcing the droop from her shoulders, coming upright in the saddle. 'The sooner we see the end of this hell-hole the better, Jack.'

Jack Danner was both pleased and worried by Sarah's response; pleased not to have to pause, and worried that Sarah might be pushing herself beyond endurance. Were she to do so and pass out, the break in their journey could be a whole lot longer than would be healthy. In the last hour, he had seen several dust clouds, some way off. But there was smoke again rising from the hilltops, and obviously the Indian trouble was far from over.

A short way on, coming on a burning wagon with the scent of fresh blood in the air, the threat from the Apaches became all too real. Sarah swayed in her saddle on seeing a man lying close to the wagon, his innards spilling out through the slit in his belly. There was evidence of a woman's presence in the female garments scattered around in the pillaged debris, but the woman's body was nowhere to be seen, which meant that the Indian bucks had taken her prisoner.

A fate a whole lot worse than mere death.

'There's nothing we can do here,' Danner said harshly. 'The water-hole we're headed for is only a hop-skip-and-jump from here.'

Dazed by the horror she had witnessed, Sarah Bonnington nodded compliantly. Danner rode ahead, his eyes scanning every inch of the uneven terrain that provided cover for any Indians who might still be on the prowl, right up to the second he and Sarah would come face to face with them, which would be way too late.

Danner took his sixgun from his holster and cocked it, not to kill an Indian, should he appear, but rather to use the single shot he'd get off to save Sarah the ordeal of falling alive into Apache captivity.

As he drew near to the water-hole, Danner dismounted and instructed Sarah to do likewise, and then approached as if walking on eggs. Buzzards were watching from the higher perches around the basin in which the waterhole was situated, and that was not a good sign. Vultures had an uncanny sense of a meal in the offing. They were already bloated with feasting, but that would not deter the foul critters from feasting some more.

He listened intently for any sound of

voices or movement coming from the water-hole and heard nothing, and maybe that was the problem — the desert stillness was too intense. Expectant, one of those fancy dime-novel writers would say. What to do with Sarah, that was Jack Danner's problem. Leave her to wait until he went and checked out the water-hole? Maybe she wouldn't be around when he got back. Or take her with him, and walk smack into trouble? Danner thought that he had never had as many dilemmas as he'd had in the hard ride to Largo.

He decided on going on alone. Sarah did not receive the news well.

'Be back before you know I'm gone,' he said soothingly.

Fortunately there was some scraggly brush to use as cover from the direction he was approaching. He crouched as close to the ground as possible, and monitored the water-hole from a hillock. The water-hole seemed empty of any presence, but then it would be if there was anyone there who did not want to be seen until they were good and ready. And there was only one way to flush them out, and that was to show himself.

Taking a couple of deep breaths, Danner stood up.

He tensed, expecting a bullet or an arrow to pierce him. But when the still calm remained so, his wariness eased a little, but not too much. On his way down the slope to the water-hole, he remained alert and ready to dive for cover. When he reached it, he found the woman, huddled and insane. Seeing him she flew at Danner, her nails clawing at him like talons. So rabid was her anger that he struggled to hold her off and calm her.

'I don't mean you any harm, ma'am,' he reassured her several times before her eyes began to lose their madness. She fell to the ground weeping, spent.

Danner did not have to wonder very long about why the woman was still alive. She had not served her purpose fully which meant that the Indians who had taken her were close by and coming back. Or word had been passed to another party of bucks. The Apaches would know that there would be little risk of losing the woman. If she tried to escape, how far could she get? They knew every inch of their domain and would easily run her to ground.

'Wait,' he told her. The woman clung to him, dragging him back as he tried to leave. 'I'll be back. There's a woman with me.' Danner tore himself away. The woman began to wail in anguish. He could not let her be, caterwauling as she was. He beckoned and she again clung to him. 'We must hurry,' he said.

When the distraught woman saw Sarah she immediately sought her solace, which was unstinting. Though not unsympathetic, Danner was conscious of seconds ticking; seconds that could mean the difference between life and death. Sarah, sensing his unease, got the woman on board one of the spare horses which he had inherited from Lucky Moreno, and they returned to the water-hole, relieved that the water had not been fouled by man or beast. It was not the sweetest water Danner had drunk, but it surely was the most welcome.

'We're going to make it, Jack,' Sarah said enthusiastically. 'I just feel it in my bones.'

Despite his heavy burden of worry, Danner laughed.

'Your bones ain't near old enough, Sarah,' he chuckled.

Sarah Bonnington stretched.

'They've aged a great deal these last two days, Jack Danner,' she said.

He filled the canteens, and began the steeper climb into the sharply rising hills, the feeling of being watched still haunting him.

20

Having finally decided to come their way, the storm broke in the late afternoon, bringing with it premature darkness. Danner welcomed its cover, but cursed its inconvenience. The storm caught them on a narrow section of the trail bordering a ravine. The deluge sped down on them from the rising ground above, uprooting trees and dislodging boulder, rock and shale, making it necessary to continually dodge. Gushing water swept away great chunks from the edge of the trail, narrowing it even further. There was also the danger that the trail would crumble underfoot and pitch them into the ravine and certain death. He might have some chance of pulling his horse out of any waywardness, however, Sarah, an inexperienced rider in the hostile terrain, would have her fate sealed before she realized the danger. The woman he did not know about. The contents of the wagon had pointed to its owners being sodbusters and not ranchers, therefore her skill with a horse would be behind a plough and not riding.

The torrent rushing off the higher ground was growing ever more fierce. In no time at all, they would be swept right off the hills. The horses, too, were getting edgy and more difficult to control. Dazzled by lightning they might bolt. Therefore, it was with immense relief that Danner saw the shack in a wooded clearing off the trail, which he immediately headed for. Nearing the shack he heard drunken giggling. He held his hand in the air for Sarah and the woman to halt. He indicated to them to dismount as silently as possible and take cover. The raging storm probably made that unnecessary, but Danner could see no point in risking being heard.

He crept up on to the shack and

edged up to the window. The grime on the window was impenetrable, and he had to risk wiping a patch of it off to see inside the shack. There were two Apache bucks lying on the floor, several whiskey bottles, probably pillaged from the sodbusters' wagon were scattered about.

They'd pose no problem.

However, Sarah's shout of warning heralded a problem. He swung around just in time to duck the swinging tomahawk. The Indian was tipsy, but not drunk. Danner niftily side-stepped the Apache and swung a boot into the Indian's groin. Being off balance, the kick lost most of its venom, but had sufficient momentum left to poleaxe the Apache. The buck doubled and howled in pain. Danner heard shuffling from inside the shack. The bucks inside were drunk, but their comrade's scream of agony might cut through their drunken haze. The woman was now screaming fit to burst her lungs, her horror reawakened by the sight of the Indian.

Sarah muffled the woman's screams as best she could. Danner had to silence the Apache quickly. He used the tomahawk which the Apache had dropped to nurse his injury, to split open the buck's skull. The shack door was opening. Danner sprang to the side of the door. The first Indian staggered out, his eyes swimming. Danner used the tomahawk on him also. The other Indian had sobered enough to avoid Danner's lunge. The tomahawk flew from his grasp. He spun around to face the furious knife-wielding Apache. Danner was tempted to simply shoot the Indian. The fury of the storm would probably muffle the gunfire, but the wind could also carry it to enemy ears. He reckoned that the three bucks had left the main party to slug whiskey, but betting on that was a risky business.

The blade of the Indian's knife flashed across his face as Danner danced away. The Apache followed through, but the liquor in him reached his legs and he wobbled wildly. Danner hit him hard on the side of the head. The Indian staggered back, shaking his head to clear his vision. Danner followed through quickly, giving the buck no time to regain his wits. He grabbed his wrist and forced the knife into his gut. The Indian tried to pull it out, but Danner rammed it in to the hilt. The Apache slumped to the ground, whimpered like a wounded animal, rolled over and lay still.

Sarah and the woman ran to the shack, but Danner quickly redirected them to the cover of a clutch of spindly pine nearby.

'We wait here for a spell,' he said.

'Mary's in pretty bad shape, Jack,' Sarah said, comforting the woman. 'She needs to get inside, fast.'

'It won't do her much good to be inside the shack if Indians come looking,' he said, unsympathetically. 'We wait for an hour.'

'An hour!' Sarah complained.

'An hour,' Danner repeated sternly. 'And don't give me no sass, Sarah!'

'I'll be fine,' the woman reassured Sarah. 'Your man is right. I'd rather be cold out here, than dead in there.'

'My man?' Sarah yelped. 'Have you lost your senses completely, Mary?'

So vehement was Sarah Bonnington's renunciation of Mary's assertion that Jack Danner reckoned that the Jack in Sarah's dreams, was indeed some wealthy young Boston tyro.

Mary smiled weakly, but knowingly.

'I guess you just don't know it yet, Sarah, huh?' she said.

Danner relented after half an hour and they went inside the shack. Its stench was overpowering, but shelter from the storm was welcome. For the second night running, there was no question of sleep for Danner, and by morning every muscle in his body ached.

'Once we reach the summit and start down the other side, it won't take long to reach Largo,' he told Sarah, when she expressed her concern about his physical state. 'I reckon our troubles are over now. Soon you'll be with your pa.'

His prediction of a trouble-free journey to Largo seemed set to be proved correct until, a couple of miles from Largo, riding through a small canyon, his prediction went out the window. At the same time that they found the man called Ben, Bonnington's stage driver dying by the side of the trail, a knife protruding from his chest, Spencer Bonnington and his second henchman put in an appearance, both brandishing rifles. On seeing them, Jack Danner understood the feeling of being watched, and a whole lot more.

'Uncle Spencer,' Sarah hailed her uncle joyfully. Danner grabbed her reins to stop her riding to meet Bonnington. 'What're you doing, Jack. Let go of my reins.'

Spencer Bonnington's laughter was ugly.

'I shouldn't have hired someone so smart as you, Danner,' Bonnington said. 'Ben got conscience, so I had to take care of him.'

'What are you talking about, Uncle Spencer?' Sarah asked, puzzled.

Confused, she looked to Danner for an explanation of her uncle's nasty mood.

'I reckon you were never meant to reach Largo, Sarah,' he said. 'Ain't that so, Bonnington?'

'It surely is,' Spencer Bonnington admitted, confident in his ability to counter any threat to his plans. 'You see, Sarah, honey, good old Uncle Spencer's fortunes haven't been good of late. In fact, I'm almost broke.'

'But you're one of Boston's wealthiest men,' Sarah said.

'Was one of Boston's wealthiest men,' Spencer Bonnington sighed. 'But, you see, Sarah, I've had a run of bad luck. And that's all it takes to make a wealthy man poor.'

'But you'll be OK. You'll make back the money you've lost, won't you?'

'The thing is, you've got to have money to make money,' Bonnington groaned.

'I'll ask Father to help, Uncle Spencer.'

'That's very kind, Sarah, but — '

'It's not help you want, is it, Bonnington?' Jack Danner interjected. 'It's every cent that your brother's got. Ain't that so?'

'Clever gent, Danner,' Bonnington said. 'What you say is true. I'll need every nickel your father's got, Sarah, to even have a chance of regaining my fortunes. When I got word that your father was dying, it was the break I'd been looking for to avoid financial ruin and disgrace.'

'I don't understand, Uncle Spencer,' Sarah said.

'Tell her, Danner,' Bonnington said. 'I'm sure you have it all figured out by now.'

'Jack . . . ?' Sarah pleaded.

Danner explained.

'When your father dies, you're his only child and heir, Sarah. You'll inherit everything. But with you out of the way,' — his look at Spencer Bonnington was contemptuous — 'he'll become your father's only heir and get every dime.'

Sarah Bonnington's shock was total.

'You know, Danner,' Bonnington said, 'pity I have to kill you. I could do with a clever gent like you back in Boston.'

'You killed the Indian woman and boy,' Danner stated.

'You gave me the idea back in Haley Ridge when we were talking about Indian trouble, Danner. So I started some, in the hope that I wouldn't have to do what I now must do,' Spencer Bonnington said. 'I figured that you'd never make it through Indian territory alive. And Sarah's death would be down to those savages.'

'You've had good folk slaughtered, Bonnington,' Jack Danner said grimly. 'You'll hang for that.'

'The dead don't talk, Danner,' he snorted.

'No, they don't,' he agreed. Danner settled a steady, steely gaze on Spencer

Bonnington's remaining henchman. 'Bonnington won't want any witnesses, fella. Like he said, the dead don't talk.'

The henchman shot Bonnington a suspicious look.

'Frank is like a son to me,' Spencer Bonnington said.

'No one can leave here alive, except you, Bonnington,' Danner stated. 'That's the only way you can be sure of keeping your dark and murderous deeds secret.'

The man called Frank shifted uneasily in his saddle, and gave Bonnington an even deeper look of suspicion.

'Makes sense, Frank,' Danner said. 'You know it does.'

'The way you tell it makes sense, sure enough, Danner,' Frank growled.

'Can't you see what Danner's trying to do?' Bonnington said. 'He's trying to divide and conquer. Haven't I always looked after you, Frank?'

'Like you looked after Ben, just now?' Sarah said.

'Ben didn't have the guts to do what

needed to be done, when the Indians didn't do it for him,' Bonnington fumed.

He shifted slightly sideways in his saddle. The movement was barely noticeable, neither was the merest realignment of Bonnington's rifle. However, Jack Danner recognized his intent.

'Look out, Frank,' he shouted, too late.

Bonnington's rifle cracked and ripped a hole in his henchman's side. Danner leapt on Bonnington and they went tumbling to the ground. Spencer Bonnington's skull crunched against a jagged rock, a long, narrow point of which poked through Bonnington's right eye. Bile rose up Jack Danner's throat.

'I'll go and see my father now, Jack,' Sarah said, matter-of-factly. 'I'll send a crew to bury my uncle where he belongs. Right here.'

The woman who would boss her father's ranch was evident in that moment.

'Sure, ma'am,' Jack Danner said.

It was a week later. Nathaniel Bonnington had died, happy that he had spent his last hours and days with his daughter, waiting for his brother Spencer to arrive from Boston. Sarah saw no point in revealing her uncle's treachery. When the funeral was over, Sarah made the journey to a town twenty miles distant, from where word had reached her that Jack Danner was getting rich in the annual cattlemen's poker extravaganza, using the $1500 she had insisted on paying him as a stake. She reckoned that Danner would not now be interested in working for her, but he might be interested in another proposition she had in mind. It was a bold and a brazen thing for a woman to propose to a man, but she figured that if she did not propose to Jack Danner, she'd be old and bent before he got round to it.

When she reached town, she was taken aback by the quietness of the saloon, where the annual poker extravaganza was held.

'Poker's done with, ma'am,' the

barkeep told her. 'Until this time next year, that is.'

'There was a gentleman by the name of Danner. Jack Danner.'

'Gone.'

'Gone?' Sarah Bonnington's heart lurched. 'Gone where?'

The barkeep shrugged. 'He's a saddletramp, ma'am.'

'But the men out at the ranch said that Mr Danner was set to scoop every cent.'

'Craziest thing I ever seen,' the barkeep said, his eyes glowing with recollection. 'Ten thousand dollars he put into that final pot.' He rolled his eyes and began to wipe the bar with a bar cloth. 'Yes, ma'am. Craziest thing I ever seen.'

On coming from the saloon, Sarah Bonnington looked to the winding trail at the end of the main street, leading out of town — the trail Jack Danner would have taken. Her heart went along that trail with him, and would on every trail thereafter. Someday, he might find his way back to Largo, and she would be waiting.

Until then, she had a ranch to run.

THE END

We do hope that you have enjoyed reading this large print book.

Did you know that all of our titles are available for purchase?

We publish a wide range of high quality large print books including:
Romances, Mysteries, Classics
General Fiction
Non Fiction and Westerns

Special interest titles available in large print are:
The Little Oxford Dictionary
Music Book, Song Book
Hymn Book, Service Book

Also available from us courtesy of Oxford University Press:
Young Readers' Dictionary
(large print edition)
Young Readers' Thesaurus
(large print edition)

For further information or a free brochure, please contact us at:
Ulverscroft Large Print Books Ltd.,
The Green, Bradgate Road, Anstey,
Leicester, LE7 7FU, England.
Tel: (00 44) **0116 236 4325**
Fax: (00 44) **0116 234 0205**

FIND MADIGAN!

Hank J. Kirby

Bronco Madigan was the top man in the US Marshals' Service — and now he was missing. Working on the most important and most dangerous mission he'd ever been assigned, he'd disappeared into the gunsmoke. Everything pointed to him being one of the many dead bodies left along the bloody trail. Even his sidekick, Kimble, was almost ready to give up the search, but the Chief's orders were very clear: 'Find Madigan . . . at all costs!'